THE REBEL DIDN'T HESITATE. HE JABBED THE RED GUARD IN THE THROAT, CUTTING OFF HIS WARNING SHOUT.

The young Chinese soldier gurgled and died. Grabbing him by his belt, the Tibetan rebel hurled him off the balcony.

Bart Lasker leaned over and watched as the guard's body fell through a layer of clouds surrounding the top of the mountain down into the abyss below.

Without a word, Lasker and his men proceeded toward the singled barred window on the far wall. As they did so, Lasker noted the wind-worn friezes embossed on the walls of the dark fortress—ancient, gruesome depictions of obscene rituals: Robed figures circling about a great fire coming through the floor of a pillared temple, a huge statue with human body parts piled high before it. This place had been a *Bonpo* stronghold.

Lasker shuddered. The smell of evil seemed to reek here. His highly attuned senses picked up a sickening stench. He sniffed the thin air. Sweat and fear. And there, beyond the bars—intense pain.

THE EXECUTIONER
by Don Pendleton

Available wherever paperbacks are sold, or order direct from the Publisher. Send cover price plus 50¢ per copy for mailing and handling to Pinnacle Books, Dept. 17-307, 475 Park Avenue South, New York, N.Y. 10016. Residents of New York, New Jersey and Pennsylvania must include sales tax. DO NOT SEND CASH.

MYSTIC REBEL V

Ryder Syvertsen

PINNACLE BOOKS
WINDSOR PUBLISHING CORP.

PINNACLE BOOKS

are published by

Windsor Publishing Corp.
475 Park Avenue South
New York, NY 10016

First printing: January, 1990

Printed in the United States of America

Introduction

The greatest and longest running mass murder of all times was engineered by one man: China's Communist leader Chairman Mao Tse Tung. Chairman Mao set in motion the slaughter of fifty million of his own people—a slaughter capped by the so-called Cultural Revolution. This final phase of the exterminations was the deliberate destruction of everything old and valued within China's borders. And since Tibet had been conquered by China's army in the 1950's and was considered part of China, the destruction spread there as well. Indeed, it was more complete and ruthless in Tibet, for there was much of value there to destroy.

When Red China invaded Tibet in the 1950's, the People's Liberation Army (PLA) began a systematic "erasal" of the ancient system of Buddhist learning and culture that had existed for a thousand years in Tibet. Tibet's six thousand huge monastaries, its innumerable temples, the very *soul* of Tibet was to be erased. It had to be eliminated and replaced, said Mao, by a new order that deified Mao and his pathetically shallow "great thoughts." Once the monasteries—some as large as small cities—were burned and dynamited, drably uniformed stone-eyed occupation "leaders" began teaching the antihuman doctrine of Communist orthodoxy to replace the spiritual beliefs of the Tibetans. The PLA leaders stood in the ruins and waved *The Little Red Book,* the book of collection sayings, in the Tibetan people's faces. These thoughts of Mao were to replace poetry, religion, art—life itself.

But no one believed this little red book! During the spontaneous mass revolt of the Tibetan people in 1959, rocks and sticks were pitted against tanks and machine guns. Two hundred thousand Tibetans lost their lives in nine days. Then followed mass arrests, deliberate starvation of whole segments of the population—the systematic incendiary destruction of the ancient culture of wisdom and compassion. The medical texts—full of cures for all diseases—were burned. The ancient manuscripts describing ancient visits by space travelers to the "roof of the world" were likewise set to the torch. A few books were hidden, a few were spirited away to India. But the world had suffered a loss that could never be regained.

In the aftermath of the revolt, all of Tibet's holy lamas—Tibetan religious leaders—were considered to be "American agents" (though most had never heard of the United States). They were condemned to execution by being buried alive, torn apart, crushed by tanks, or crucified. The road to Lhasa, capital of Tibet, was lined with crucified lamas for months. And all citizens of Tibet, which was now totally absorbed into China and renamed Xijian, the "west-

6

ern treasure house," were told they must conform. They must cease to believe in anything except Communist doctrine. All Xijianese must work hard now, said the authorities, to build the Chinese military roads that lead to India, the *next*, but not the last, conquest for the Chinese People's Liberation Army.

Sullen Tibetans, under the gun, had little choice. They dug the deep cuts in their magnificent mountains so that the Chinese tanks might pass. They ate the stale, wormy leftovers of the Communist occupiers. And they waited for the tide to turn. For they knew the hope of freedom still lived. They knew their God-King the Dalai Lama was yet alive. Through the heroic efforts of thousands, the Dalai Lama, the head of state of Tibet, had escaped to India, along with a hundred thousand Tibetans, before the border became ringed with iron.

The slaughter of the Tibetan people, the pall of death and destruction caused by China in the "Forbidden Kingdom" has not gotten much publicity in a war-weary world. Few statesmen, in this era of reconciliation, speak loudly of the Tibetan holocaust, which the Tibetans have come to call The Replacement. Perhaps the world has been lulled because of the first Chinese attack on India, in the 1960's, which fizzled. It was stalled by fanatical Ghurka troops, backed by a resolute Indian government. The Chinese expected many Indians to welcome them, expected the front to collapse. But it didn't. The Indian people backed their government, knowing what happened to Tibet—hearing the eyewitness accounts of the Tibetan exiles. That resolute stand—plus internal problems in China—stayed the Communist sweep south.

The attack on India was rescheduled, postponed until the mid-1990's. India had been temporarily spared, but the slaughter, The Replacement, continued inside the wall of silence and steel that ringed Tibet . . .

Mao is no longer with us, and many of his policies have been repudiated. Eventually, many of his accomplices were put on trial and executed—even Mao's actress wife was given a long prison sentence. But all is not well in the Middle Kingdom. Reforms are paper thin. Any spark of democracy or freedom, like the student occupation of Beijing's central square, are dealt with by tanks and machine guns. The Communists continue the veneration of Mao's image. The new leaders say that Mao didn't really know about the "problems" his policies caused, and that he did a lot of good things, too. The new leaders adopt "capitalist incentives," and talk of "eventual" democratization. And they ask for and get new helicopters and artillery from the United States to strengthen their occupation army.

While the world is lulled into sleep, the Communists continue the settlement and exploitation of the last unspoiled place on earth—Tibet. The seven million Tibetans now have been given strict quotas on birth rates, with severe punishment mandated for any Tibetan woman who has more than one child. Meanwhile, ten million Chinese nationals are being moved onto Tibetan soil. The Tibetans are now a minority in their own nation. They will soon become, like the Indians of America's West, a passed-by leftover of the past, an unpleasant annoyance to be swept away bit by bit. Or so the Communists believe.

But over the years there arose strange rumors, tales

whispered at night, tales about a great avenger who had appeared in the West. The stories grew into legends and gave hope. A man had appeared, a man whom it had been prophesied was a "mystic rebel," a great force who would bring freedom to Tibet, even as the rest of the world fell down into tyranny for seven hundred years of darkness.

This is where our story begins. The year: 1990. An American adventurer, Bart Lasker, flew into Chinese-held Tibet and was shot down. Thus prophesies started to be fulfilled: Lasker was held captive by a race of ancient sorcerers atop a strange mountain called the Hidden Realm. And in that bizarre mountain aerie Lasker acquired—or rather *stole*—vast and mysterious powers and escaped. The die was cast. Fate has dictated that Bart Lasker, an American who just a few years earlier hadn't even heard of Tibet, would become intimately involved in the Tibetan struggle. His karma had determined that he would be involved in the greater struggle as well—a fight against an unimaginable evil that now looms like a black hand over the whole world.

Living in Dharmsala India—the exile capital of the Tibetan diaspora—Lasker studies the arcane methods of Tibetan medicine—including the cures for the "seven new diseases." But his studies are often interrupted. He must lay aside his peaceful studies and heed the call to action. He is called upon again to fulfill the ancient prophesies: In order that Tibet will live again and be the light of the world in the Time of Ultimate Darkness, the powers of the Mystic Rebel, must once more be unleashed.

Prologue

The twisting black clouds roiled and thundered as they rushed between the ice-clad sheer cliffs of the Tibetan mountains. The freezing cold, dark winds howled, and hailstones pelted the peaks. The tallest of the mountains, the one designated on the Chinese military maps as K-5, was a snag tooth-shaped black basalt tombstone. Its slopes were nearly vertical on all sides. It seemed the least likely place on earth to be inhabited, but it was.

The storm that lashed through the Himalayan range had been blowing all night. Now, the first faint light of gray winter dawn revealed that ten-foot-high ice dunes had been created against a low-slung artificial structure perched two-thirds of the way up K-5's twenty-three-thousand-foot height. Only the uppermost of the three-story structure was free of the white mass.

This gray granite building was the Fortress of Despair, a forbidding ancient ruin of a temple to Drugah, a fierce god not worshipped in Buddhist Tibet for a thousand years. The fortress had been abandoned for centuries, but recently it had been reoccupied, repaired. And the slitlike windows in the age-old walls now had a new addition: steel bars. This place that oozed a feeling of long-ago evil was now a maximum security prison run by the Chinese Communists. It held those Tibetan freedom fighters who were singled out by the occupation army of Red China as being especially dangerous, prisoners who had to serve the hardest of hard time.

The screams of the lost souls crying out from behind those cold steel bars echoed through the mountains every day, audible for a hundred miles. It was a sound to chill the bones of the few solitary yak herders who traversed this remote area with their small herds.

Now, as the red sun broke over the peaks to the west, the screams began again. As yellow streamers like banners broke through the storm clouds, a giant Himalayan eagle leapt from its high nest as if in response to the cries of pain. Twisting and buffeted by the wind, the eagle rode the fierce winds and soared high over the dismal evil building, scraping at the clouds. The bird cried out, a single, mournful sharp note. It was as if that magnificent eight-foot wingspan creature sensed the pain inside those ice-battered walls, sensed the despair, and smelled the death. The eagle dove toward the structure and only at the last second pulled out of its dive and, rocking its huge wings, flew away. It had given its tribute. A salute to the eagle's fellow countrymen, a tribute to those poor souls whose only crime was to value freedom as much as the eagle did. Then, flapping its mighty wings hard, it flew south.

In the uppermost—and coldest—cell of Prison K-5, a beautiful raven-haired woman lay naked, shivering on a thin floor pallet. She lay under a single thin wool army blanket and shook and listened to the screams. It was the screams that awakened her like a reliable alarm clock each and every morning. A few minutes later she would be fed. Then she would wait for the Chinese officers to come again—to intimidate her, to question her, to threaten her.

Dorjee Nyima was the woman's name, if she had a name any longer. She had been confined in this bitterly cold cell for over a month now. Because she was a freedom-fighter. Because she had defied the occupiers of her once-independent land. One month of interrogation, one month of rancid food, one month of shivering under the filthy blanket. And yet she had not broken. Dorjee was proud of that. Proud that she had not revealed any names. But she knew their practices. Soon the Communists would switch over from intimidation, discomfort, poor food. They would go on to the next step—degradation. Her rape was inevitable. Then would come the instruments designed to produce ultimate pain. And she would scream. Dorjee would scream like all the others. And eventually she would tell what she knew. Fortunately, that wasn't much. The resistance fighters were organized into three- or four-person units. They had no idea of the larger plans of their leaders, only the unit's part in the struggle.

How long, she thought, *until I lose my mind?*

There had been symptoms already: Dorjee had

been seeing things — hallucinations. Mostly they had come in the stygian, icy darkness. Figures — green-glowing figures had moved around her pallet, staring down at her with catlike eyes, staring from green-hooded robes. Icy skeleton fingers had seemed to point at her, ghostly faint laughter had wafted through the blackness. So it had been last night. The images of the corpse-beings had come. And she had driven the bad images away with mantras, invoked the name of Buddha, Chenresig, Manjushri. And then she had formed in her mind's eye the image of her lover, the American Bart Lasker, whom the fates had kept her from seeing for two years now. Dorjee had envisioned his smiling face, imagined Bart's strong arms holding her, comforting her. It was an image so strong that eventually the green figures dematerialized.

In a warm, soundproof, fire-lit room in another part of the Fortress of Despair, another person sat bolt upright in his downy soft bed. He was gasping, sucking in air that seemed reluctant to enter his lungs. And when General Zin Xiao was able to breathe, he still had the feeling of the suffocating claw-hand in his dream. It still seemed to grasp at his throat.

Sweating profusely, the sloe-eyed Chinese officer threw off his quilt cover and went to the sink. He threw hot water into his face, and then stared into the mirror. His eyes were bloodshot. Again. He ate well, he had good quarters, and he was in charge of a hundred elite officers. He tried to tell himself this, tried to believe that everything was all right — but was

14

it? Why was he, of all the generals, sent to this forsaken place near Beijing? Had he not led the glorious Fifteenth Unit into Tianamen Square last year and dealt with the student protestors with dispatch. Had he not commanded his reluctant troops to roll their tanks over those demonstrators for democracy? Was it not *his* hand on the throttle of the tank that had toppled the despicable Goddess of Democracy statue the students had erected facing Chairman Mao's glorious hundred-foot-high portrait? Yes it was! Then why? Why must he be here in this frozen hell? And why did that nightmare always come? Why was the claw-hand of Death grasping at his throat?

A knock at the door pulled Zin away from these thoughts. It was his orderly, Sergeant Wang Zi, of course. Still, the knock startled Zin. He shouted, "I am not ready, I must shave."

With shaking hand, he picked up the straight razor and stared at it. The gleam of the overhead light on its edge made him feel nauseated. Still, he took his shaving mug out of the cabinet and began to lather up. He smiled. Today, phase two would begin with the special woman prisoner. Today it would be more than just words, more than just threats. She was a beauty, this one. And she was his for the taking. And when he had satisfied the simpler of his needs on her body, then the more exquisite pleasures would begin. He had a taste for that. They didn't call Zin the Beijing Butcher without reason. Many a student democracy demonstrator had learned new hard lessons at the sharp end of Zin's scalpel or his small steel drills. And they had begged, pleaded, aroused him. They had told all they knew and done all he requested.

15

Of course, this Dorjee Nyima *could* be innocent. The wrong person had been arrested more than once. But even if she knew nothing, she was guilty. Because the orders from Beijing were explicit. She was guilty. The People are always right. The representatives of the People don't make mistakes. Truth, after all, is relative, Zin thought, as he slid the razor down along his pockmarked right cheek, removing hard, dry stubble. The will of the people, said Chairman Mao, *creates* truth. The woman would be kept here at the fortress and interrogated and tortured because truth is relative. The People said she was guilty. That was enough.

Chapter One

The only sound in the great room of the Dharmsala Library was the turning of pages. A dozen men in western priests' garb sat in booths of maplewood and teak, each studying English translations of the ancient text. The text itself was on display a dozen feet in front of the rows of booths.

If the priests and pastors looked up they could easily see the three silver scroll cases — and the roll of yellowed manuscripts they had contained — pressed behind bullet-proof vacuum glass alongside them. Though brilliantly lit by spotlights, the parchments were displayed in special nonfading lighting to prevent their faint but discernible words from further fading.

The object of all this research was the archaeological find of the century: the St. Thomas texts, dating from 50 C.E. The missing Fifth Gospel!

There was one man sitting in an isolated booth in the rear of the library not dressed as a priest. He was tall and tan; an outdoor man. His name was Bart Lasker and he was the renegade pilot who had brought back the three scrolls last year from the forbidding mountains to the north.

The ex-CIA odd-jobber had been going to the library every day for a month, right after his noontime Aryvedic medicine class, and reading his discovery.

Today he finished reading the entire translation from Aramaic into Tibetan. Lasker was as fluent in Tibetan as if it were his native language. He had been able to read it ever since his extraordinary experience in a Bon monastery in Tibet, an experience that forever changed him into a powerful warrior with powers far beyond mere mortal dimensions. This transformation had bewildered him at first and led him to seek the advice and guidance of a mountain hermit in Tibet. The hermit had told Bart Lasker he would become the champion of the cause of Tibetan freedom. And he did.

The brown-eyed six-foot-plus, heavily muscled man looked out of place among the pasty-faced priests, many with gray hair. Lasker's hair was shoulder-length, shiny dark brown. As he finished the readings, he sighed heavily and stared ahead at the illuminated scrolls. He was deeply moved to have read the missing words of Jesus, recorded by the disciple Thomas. This hitherto unknown teaching of the man who had been thought to have died on the cross, but who had actually lived on in India, was an awesome marvel. Lasker leaned back in the comfortable swivel chair and looked around at the scholars, each bent over their English language translations — just Tibetan and English copies for now, but eventually the scrolls would be translated into all languages. And the controversy would spread.

This room of the library on Dharmsala was magnificent, Lasker thought. It looked like something that had been there for centuries—the teak-carved paneling, the sacred art tapestries—but he knew it was all built in the last twenty years by the exiled people of Tibet who settled down in this northernmost province of India. This was the most elaborate of the three-story library's rooms—and why not? It had been refurbished recently, in large part by the use of monies donated by several Christian churches, whose hierarchies had decided that the Thomas texts deserved a decent place! They were *real*. Lasker, above all, knew that for a fact! He stood up and stretched, feeling sore and out of shape. He vowed that he would get back to his heavy regimen of E-Kung martial arts exercise; and practice diligently the yogis' *asana* postures that he had missed for the past month. He picked up the text copy and brought it to the desk. The monk boy clerk took it reverently and covered it in red satin cloth, then put it back on a shelf.

Lasker yawned, walked to the cloakroom down the hallway, took his red nylon Arctic parka off the hook, and then strode out to the double doors of the library entrance.

When he opened the second door, he felt a blast of frigid air. He zipped up his parka tight and let his eyes adjust to the wintry darkness. It was near midnight; the exile capital was shut down. He could just barely see one single electric bulb and the neon-flashing red sign ahead. That would be Tranga's Tattoo Palace. He sighted the snowy path he wanted glowing red from the neon, started down the steps. Between the crunching steps of his boots on the snow, Lasker heard distant voices — singing. Christmas carols? Of course! It was Christmas Eve! He reached the bottom step and took in several deep breaths. The icy air invigorated him, reminded him of his much-loved adopted homeland — Tibet. Tibet, the mysterious land whose gleaming ice towers were visible over the Dalai Lama's exile palace now, reflecting their ghostly glow on the smooth ice of the pond in front of his new two-story palace.

He heard the library door open behind him and the surprised gasp. He turned to see a gray-haired man in a black wool coat quickly wrap a scarf around his neck, then pull on thick mittens. An elderly priest who looked familiar . . . Yes he recognized him! Father Heimlin from Germany.

Bart touched the shoulder of the priest when he came down alongside him. Heimlin was startled. "Oh, Lasker" — (he knew nothing of Bart's other identity) — "It is so dark, I didn't see you. How goes the reading?"

"I'm finished."

"Ah, finished just in time for Christmas?"

"Yes" Lasker returned the smile. "Kind of fitting, isn't it? I'd forgotten the date. There are no Christmas trees up in this Buddhist community, no wreaths. I haven't observed Christmas for a long time. For as long as I've lived here — four years."

"Oh, you're a Buddhist?" The smile remained, though it seemed forced.

"Of a sort . . ."

"Well, whatever your religion, would you share some hot brew with an old priest?"

"Sure," Lasker smiled. "I'd love to." He had

planned to go straight to the house at forty-three Duernapas Alley where he lived. But what the hell—it was Christmas and he had spoken to few westerners in the last months. Sleep could wait.

As they walked abreast on the winding path, Lasker wondered who had shoveled in the middle of the night to make their journey easier.

The priest engaged him in conversation, which soon took an argumentative direction. "Do you still actually believe the document is authentic?"

"Yes," Lasker said dryly. "I believe so." He didn't elaborate.

"Ah, maybe so, maybe so," the priest said, pulling his earmuffs over his ears. "But there are those who say it is not really 1,940 years old, but rather that the scrolls date from a later period—written on older paper with old ink. That's why the carbon-14 dating tests would come out right on the button."

"What do you think, Father?" Lasker asked, his breath making clouds.

"I don't know, myself," he puffed, "I haven't decided . . . You know, my bishop is a skeptical man. We've seen so-called discoveries before."

"I'm convinced that these are Christ's missing words," said Lasker "and that his body is entombed—as it says at the end of the Thomas text—in Shrinigar. I'm going to Shrinigar to see the tomb of Christ in the spring. Want to come?"

The priest seemed excited at the idea. He almost giggled. "I don't know. If my superiors would—"

Suddenly little Dewap came running from behind waving a note. "Lasker, thank heaven I found you! I first went to the library—you weren't there! You must go see Losang immediately! Very important!" He waved his little pen flashlight around.

The priest smiled. "Eh—a message at midnight? Perhaps we must have our brew tomorrow?"

"I'm afraid so," Lasker said. "I'll come by your place about noon?"

"Fine!" The priest shook Lasker's hand. "How do you go about without gloves?" Then he turned down the path toward the only western-style hotel in town—the Paradise Arms.

Lasker followed the boy off toward the town's main square. They entered Great Boddhisattva Way—where the controversial lama Losang lived alone in a western-style thatched cottage that contrasted sharply with all the whitewashed stone buildings near it.

As they approached the unusual cottage, Lasker heard music. A piano. It was Losang, no doubt, banging away at his baby grand. Losang was playing *Silent Night,* with a lot of verve. *Fortissimo!*

Lasker smiled. The Tibetan holy man was much taken by the Christian religion. Almost as much as he was taken by hot English sports cars. Lasker had often heard Losang play liturgical music, including the elaborate *St. Matthew's Passion,* by Bach. Some of the other lamas feared Losang would actually convert to Christianity. But all such fears were unfounded. The rotund Losang said he had just "incorporated" Christianity into Buddhism where it fit nicely—according to this quixotic modern lama.

The music ceased, and before they reached it, the door opened, pouring candlelight out onto the pristine white snow. And a shape appeared nearly blocking the light. Losang had put on a bit more weight.

22

He was dressed in a smoking jacket.

"Ah, Lasker," Losang said. "Come in. Oh! You will have some Mongolian bread cookies and hot mulled cider. Happy Christmas. Please, come in, come in."

"Merry Christmas to you, too," Lasker said, crossing the doorsill.

The boy monk leapt inside behind Lasker and then sat down on the rug, quietly regaining his composure, staring at the cookie jar high on a shelf. Dewap was obsessed with sweets, Lasker could almost feel his excitement!

They had hot cider and cookies first. Then the tombstone-white teeth of Losang were revealed as he broke into a broad, curious smile. It was, Lasker decided, not exactly a warm smile, more like the smile of the Cheshire cat—a taunting grin. The lama reached into a pocket and handed Lasker a telegram message.

He ripped it open. It was from a man in Nepal named Norla Singh, a man who Lasker knew had many contacts in Tibet—despite the iron curtain the Communists had raised between that northern country and the outside world. The message—written in English—stated that Singh had heard something important. There was conclusive proof that Lasker's lover, Dorjee Nyima had been arrested. Singh's news was that the young doe-eyed Tibetan beauty was now being held captive of the PLA in a remote fortress prison on a mountain called K-5. She was being treated well.

Lasker leaned back exhaling a sigh of relief. When he had read that Dorjee had been arrested he had expected the telegram to go on to say she had been executed. That was the usual punishment for freedom fighters. Still, what Lasker had long feared had finally happened. Dorjee's brave service to the underground movement in Tibet had finally brought disaster.

Lasker handed back the telegram and asked, "What do you think, Losang? Can a ransom of some sort be arranged to free her? They must be aware that we would pay for her release!"

Losang shook his head. "We have already tried. Although our government has gotten many freedom fighters out of Tibet by bribery, it seems that this time they will not be bribed. I think that strange."

"I must do something!" Lasker's voice broke, betraying his anxiety.

Chapter Two

The priest, looking disturbed, placed his cup of hot cider down on the paper napkin. "I'm so sorry to hear of this trouble. I think under the circumstances, I should leave you to discuss this rather unfortunate matter."

Lasker was embarrassed. In his excitement he had utterly forgotten about the presence of Heimlin. Along with Losang, he urged the Father to stay, but not with too much vehemence. Heimlin was soon off, together with the boy, each carrying a small tin of the hot Mongolian cookies.

"I will pray that your troubles are quickly resolved," the priest said as he put on his black hat. "All will be well. Good night."

Once the priest and Dewap had left, Lonsang told Lasker, "I have anticipated your reaction since I took the liberty of opening the telegram. I have prepared for a *prasena,* a divination of the most high order. I am ready to begin. We will try together to get to the bottom of this Dorjee matter."

Lasker knew that a *prasena* was an effective tool for

finding out what was occurring, and what was likely to occur, even in the most distant places. It was a practice steeped in time, and proven throughout history. "Thank you." He really meant it.

"Thank me if it works," Losang replied. "I'm a bit rusty at this. I'm better at repairing a sports car engine, I'm afraid. I've been away from Tibet and all these occult things for too long."

The lights were extinguished save but the single thick red Tahadre candle, which produced a very bright torchlike flame a foot high. That sort of candle Lasker knew to be usually reserved for solemn occasions such as funerals or divinations.

Once the candle was lit, Losang went into the other room. He came out in a few minutes shorn of his silk smoking jacket. The rotund lama now looked very Old Tibet. Lama Losang was dressed in a saffron-colored robe glinting with threads of pure gold, its brocade mandarin-type collar studded with small shiny turquoise stones. He sat down on a pillow that faced across a black lacquer table to watch Lasker, who, as Losang had requested, had meditated silently for the moments that the high lama had been absent.

Losang adjusted his robe and took out from its hidden pockets a series of arcane objects that spoke of mystic ancient origins. The first object was a smoky quartz crystal—the kind sometimes ground up and burned in a secret method under the full moon to make an anticancer drug. Lasker had on more than one occasion helped prepare that drug in the Tibetan Astrological and Medicine Institute up the hill. This particular smoky crystal was about a foot long and six inches wide. It had five perfectly smooth sides, all coming to a point at a forty-five-degree angle at the top. As Losang recited an activating chant and waved the crystal, it glinted in the candlelight. Lasker saw, when the lama put it down on the lacquer table, that the crystal had a coating of red ochre dust on it. The red was particularly impregnated in its rough end. That, he knew, meant the crystal had been out for a week in an energy-laden meadow. That was often done so that a crystal might absorb the power of the north star. Thus prepared, such an object was a very powerful tool in the occult science of prediction.

Losang produced other objects from the folds of his robe — three copper plates, each a few inches wide. These Losang handed Lasker, who was familiar with the general outlines of *prasenas*. The Mystic Rebel placed the plates to form a triangle on the table, with about a foot of empty space in the middle.

Next the lama handed Lasker three small wooden boxes of the kind that might have contained jewelry. In this case, though, they contained the offering to the Yidams of the *Prasena* — beings in the between-worlds matrix that would assist the proceedings.

Lasker opened the boxes and poured a little of the barley, tea leaves, and salt contents within them into each copper plate. Losang picked up the crystal and swept it back and forth over the offerings, invoking the Yidams in a singsong voice.

Next the lama stood up and went to a nearby cupboard and took from it a conical container similar to the kind that chefs squeeze cream out of onto a cake. This one, however, was made of hard metal, not cardboard. The lama, by means of rubbing striations on the cone, sifted fine-grain sand onto the table. The sand was red, then by some magic, yellow, then finally white. Losang drew a sand painting in the triangular space between the bowls, completely encircling the crystal with his delicate sand symbols.

He was making a mandala, the mystic power symbol used by Tibetans to focus attention completely on some particular thought. This mandala was the reverse of most mandalas Lasker had seen. Losang had made the circle on the outside, and the square inside. He quickly drew precise symbolic depictions of the four directions and the twelve zodiac signs in the sand.

Saying the chant of invocation, the lama finished the design and then sat down and half closed hi eyes. He was as still as the dead for ten minutes or so, during which Lasker tried to remain still also, breathing shallowly.

Suddenly there was a hum. Lasker opened his eyes a bit and saw that it was a vibration emanating from the crystal—a blue glow was coming from the tip of the crystal! Slowly, ever so slowly, the crystal started to move. It soon floated up in the air an inch off the table. Then, from the tip of the crystal shot effervescent trails of slow blue fire that Tibetans called Yidam-energy. That otherworldly fire was sometimes seen in the West as well. It was the so-called faerie-fire of Scotland and Ireland, seen at the equinox time.

The glowing crystal moved in a circle in the air, sending eerie shadows flickering across the lama's cottage.

Lasker was fascinated; he had seen this particular

display of light-energy only once before—in the northern Tibetan desert. He kept his cool, not stirring from his energy-balancing lotus position. To move now might be dangerous. The blue light meant that the Yidams were here, and probably angry at being roused. They were usually angry, by nature!

He watched as Losang, bathed in the flickering light, moved his hand to the cone, spilled out some more sand to sketch in the appropriate mystic symbols of recognition. Now the sand coming out from the cone he held seemed to be blue. How did he do that? Or was it just the odd light?

The sand soon began to break out of the mandala now. All of a sudden it swirled up in the air and started spiraling around the flickering crystal.

"Now," Losang whispered, as the sand and faerie-fire danced over the mandala, "you go and get the kindling from the flint bag hanging on the refrigerator door handle! I'll keep things under control here!"

Lasker got up very quietly and did as the lama asked. He placed the pieces of twig and dry strands of hemp where Losang pointed—at all four cardinal points around the floating crystal. Then he sat down on his cushion again.

Soon the faerie-fire sent streamers like slow lightning out toward the kindling. The material caught fire, flared briefly, then each small pile of kindling died down to a glowing red, like hot charcoal. The table didn't seem to be damaged at all by these fires.

Losang again began a chant. From out of his robe he extracted a brass *varjra*-thunderbolt wand about six inches long. As he waved it, the wand started to receive the faerie-fire from the crystal. The lama

29

snapped his fingers and immediately a bell appeared in his left hand. He started to ring it at odd intervals. His chubby face, cast in shadows from below, had a serene and otherworldly expression.

Lasker had never seen Losang look this way, and it was scary. Lasker felt somehow that Losang as he knew the man, was gone! He had no personality right now; he was just an empty vessel. Lasker had been to *prasenas* before. One of particular power had been held before His Holiness the Dalai Lama himself. But never had Lasker seen this sort of blue-lightning phenomena. He was awed at the power of this very unassuming modern lama!

Losang moaned, and his head snapped back violently. He was being entered by some oracle-being, one of the participating Yidams. Losang rolled his wide head and his whole body shuddered. Then he smiled. It was not Losang's broad smile. It was a crooked sneer. The lama had, Lasker knew, become the medium for one of the Yidam-spirits contacted.

"Ask your questions, western intruder," he hissed. The voice was serpentlike, yet the words were recognizable.

"W-who are you?"

"I live in the lake-water," the voice hissed, "before the new palace of the God-king. I am not to be trifled with, so ask your questions!"

Lasker gasped. Had something gone wrong? Why was a lake-naga and not a Yidam speaking through Losang? What should he do?

Lasker was familiar with the creature some called Narl-the-Destructor. It was the fearsome lake-spirit that had once lived in a remote holy mountain lake in

Tibet, but now lived in Dharmsala. The lake-naga that now spoke with Losang's lips was shaped like an electric eel. It swam in the murky depths of the pond outside the Dalai Lama's palace, protecting him from attack, when need be, swallowing the unwary intruders.

"Go on," the naga demanded. "I know you have questions! So ask. I will reveal all that is the enemy's mind! Do not waste my time! I will destroy you if you do so!"

Chapter Three

Losang faded away, to be replaced by a five-foot-thick, slimy wet eel that had to curl and bend to fit in the cottage.

Lasker, who had faced many dangers before, felt his heart pounding. After all, this being threatening him was a most formidable otherwordly monster. Tarl was now over forty feet long — and as awful looking as anyone could imagine. A formidable naga king if ever there was one.

Lasker calmed himself enough to go on communicating by remembering the lake-naga had once been so small as to be carried to India in a bottle. Narl had been brought south from its ancestral home in the Tibetan mountains during the Chinese invasion to continue its traditional role of protecting the God-King.

He now reminded Tarl, "We are both in service to the Dalai Lama. I must ask you questions, in the interest of the cause."

There was a long pause, ended by the words, "Very well, I will do what I can to answer. But not *too* many questions."

Lasker said, "Thank you. Number one: What is going on at the prison on Widow's Claw Mountain?" His heart beat like tomtoms.

"Poor phrasing, but I understand what you wish to know! Your Dorjee is held captive by the Communists, that is true," Tarl hissed. "But they are the least of it. The Chinese Communists are manipulated by our great occult enemy, the Bonpo priest magicians, who have laid a trap for the likes of you, Bart Lasker, at that very spot."

That was a surprise. He composed a second question carefully. "How can I rescue her?"

"You will go, even if I say there is no way to succeed. Success is dependent upon more than your puny devices — it will take the protection of the Singer of the Mountain — a recluse spirit living in a monastery long in ruins. He could make the wind favor you, make the mountains not crush you. But neither you nor I control him. Be pure of purpose, be courageous and he *might* deign to protect you! Aside from the Singer of the Mountain's help, there is no chance for you or this Dorjee." A sort of laugh followed. "Lasker, success is meaningless, you should know that! The great meditator that dreams this world and all worlds into being is a *suchness*. A dream has no attributes such as success or failure!" The eel's tiny yellow eyes flickered. Its tongue, like a long ruler, darted out once.

Lasker frowned — he hated philosophy. "May I ask, Lake-naga, what specifically should I do if I wish to foil the Bonpo trap and take Dorjee from the prison unharmed?"

34

"Ah, practical matters *you* will attend to! But if you succeed, puny human, do not expect to arrive back in India too soon. There are matters greater than this rescue that will involve you. The Bonpo sorcerers who stand against all that is of the light in the world, have recently activated a vast source of power. Beware the Skull!"

"What skull?"

"Enough questions, mortal! You have received too much of my time! When all is lost, intensify the blue with the arrowhead!"

And with those words, the naga vanished. The lama shook like he was given a jolt of electricity. Losang dropped his bell and *vajra,* slumped onto the table. Instantly the faerie light faded, and the crystal tumbled over on its side. The lama's dark eyes were unfocused and wide open, like he was dead.

"Losang, are you all right?" Lasker lifted his head and slapped his face. The eyes focused. The massive mouth of tombstone teeth shone in the candlelight. A beaming smile! "I'm fine, my American friend. Was it as good for you as it was for me?"

"Be serious," Lasker complained, in great relief. "You scared me."

"Very well; what happened? Did a Yidam answer your questions?"

"I'll say! But we contacted Tarl, the lake-being."

"Really? My, my! Was he helpful?"

Lasker frowned. "Yes. And confusing." Lasker filled Losang in, ending with, "I still don't know how the Bonpo plan to trap me. The last thing Tarl said made no sense."

"Be thankful for what you did learn," Losang said,

stripping off his robe and blowing out the candle. Underneath the robe, Lasker saw, he wore red suspenders and a wide red tie with a series of Santa Clauses running on it. The lama started cleaning up. He said, "We learned that this is not just a communist versus freedom fighter situation. We have learned that the hand of the Bonpo is in this affair. And thus we are warned. *No way* should you go up there, Bart. You must bide your time and wait. They *want* you to come into their clutches. Dorjee is the bait in the trap, and you are the mouse."

Lasker sighed. Not go rescue Dorjee? He walked over to the window and drew back the curtains. They had been at it all night, he realized, for he stared out at the first light of the new day. Already the ice of the Himalayan peaks to the north glowed pale pink.

After a while he said, "The Bonpo are right, I cannot avoid going there. I will go rescue her — or die trying."

"You think you can fight through Communist soldiers *and* the Bonpo? You think you can scale the mountain called Widow's Claw? It is the sheerest mountain in Tibet. The only access to the prison is a road leading to an elevator shaft on the south face, and even that is very heavily guarded. You wouldn't make it as far as the access road!"

"Damn it! I've done the impossible more than once. I've managed, even when I *didn't* know what I was up against. This time I have the protection of His Holiness, I have my Yeshe Tsogyal amulet's power. And thanks to your *prasena,* I know what's going on. Besides, I've been working on something I think will be just the ticket for this mission. A secret weapon of a sort."

"What is it?"

"If I told you it wouldn't be a secret," Lasker said caustically. "But I'll tell you this much—it will make escaping from that mountain with Dorjee much easier. It's a high-tech device, of my own design."

Losang went over to the piano, banged a few notes, then closed the piano keyboard. "I suppose you'll go, no matter what I advise?"

Lasker nodded.

"Then I will see to it that you get help," he offered. "Our rebel friends in Tibet can be contacted. Some of the Snow Lions will be able to lend a hand." The lama started to pull the suspenders off his shoulders. "Be careful, be very careful." He yawned. "Now if you don't mind, I'm going to bed. You can sack out here on my sofa, or go home. Suit yourself."

The lama staggered into his bedroom, muttering, "Your Christmas gift is under the little tree on the piano top."

"Present?" Lasker looked over to the piano and saw the three-inch-high green pipe-cleaner wire tree, and next to it a small white box.

Lasker opened the box. Inside was a small ceramic Tibetan flag pin—red, yellow, and blue streamers coming up from a rising sun. A fitting gift for a man heading north, into the snow-locked mountains.

Lasker put it on.

Chapter Four

A month later . . .

The bright low sun was reflecting off the ice of the peak known as K-5, as if the mountain were some huge shard of mirror. Even through his deeply tinted climbers' goggles, it was too bright for Bart Lasker to be sure where he was placing his pickax. Hanging on vertical granite, at seventeen thousand feet up, you don't want to make mistakes! Lasker and his two Tibetan rebel companions—Tsering and Rinchen— had been climbing the mountain's "impossible" north face for ten hours. They were coming up on the unguarded side of the dreaded Communist prison fortress. According to information supplied by the Tibetan underground, they believed that the officers of the guard were having their supper about now—at least Lasker *hoped* they were. There were no guarantees in life.

You go with what you got . . . He gritted his teeth and planted the ax, pulled himself up another three feet.

Behind him, the other indefatigible climbers were strung together by a slender gray nylon rope, forty feet apart. They did not wear the customary bright neon parkas of mountaineers. Instead they were dressed entirely in dark gray—an effective camouflage in the gray, black, and white world of the Himalayan mountains. Even their footgear, pickaxes, and ropes were of this dull finish. Thus the intrepid adventurers were mere shadows on the windy ice-spattered escarpment. Cold, tired shadows.

There was another rope dangling taut from the waist cinch of the forward climber, a rope leading down to a ledge many feet below. The American counted upon what was at the end of that second tether to save them, once they accomplished their mission. It was his secret weapon.

Grunting and sucking in a gasp of thin air, Lasker moved his left foot to feel the rock, find a hold. Once his feet were securely placed, he lifted and dug the pickax deep once more. He pulled up another few feet, and felt the ledge. With great relief, Lasker lifted himself and rolled into the deep recess in the granite rockface. This was their last stop, their last respite, before the top.

Lasker bent low, as the indentation was barely four feet high. He tugged on the rope three times to let those below know he was okay. Looking down, the glare was not too bad. He saw Tsering wave that he understood. Both he and Rinchen seemed to quicken their upward pace. Shortly, the one-eyed rebel chieftain came up onto the ledge to join him, followed by bulky, muscular Rinchen.

They sat down, letting their feet dangle in the wind,

taking in the view. After a brief time, Lasker secured a small pulley device into the rock at the edge of the ledge with some rock screws. Then he attached the second rope through the pulley. His voice sounded tinny in the cold, thin air as he announced, "Okay, so far so good. Now give me a hand pulling up our surprise package." As the two rebels lent their muscle power to pull the rope, the pulley creaked and complained, but it held. In five minutes the six-foot-long canvas-wrapped parcel was securely on the ledge. Lasker, after making sure nothing had fallen out, said, "It's a cake walk from here, if we haven't been spotted, and provided the underground has its facts straight." Lasker tried to be optimistic!

Tsering winked his one good eye and smiled. Rinchen made the thumbs-up sign. The pair of Tibetan freedom fighters, two of Lasker's closest friends in all the world, seemed not the least bit worried. Nor were they excessively fatigued. Lasker was amazed at his own vigor as well. He hadn't felt the usual impact of high altitude. Normally he developed a splitting headache at these lofty heights. But this time, he had asked for help. Cheojey Lama, the spry octogenarian medical lama who now waited with their horses some miles away from this mountain, had supplied Lasker with certain herbal drugs — a miraculous ancient medicinal tea for climbers.

Lasker had joined up with the Snow Lion rebels near the border, on the other side of the ancient tunnel from Kasmir into Tibet. A tunnel as yet undiscovered by the Chinese Communist occupiers of the Precious Snowland of high lamas. Then they had traveled by horseback, disguised as holy pilgrims, across a thousand miles of Tibet, showing false papers to surly Peoples Liberation Army soldiers. The papers were not up to date. Only through the spell-casting ability of Cheojey Lama—the binding and confusing spells—were they able to make it to Widow's Claw Mountain. On the way, they had passed the frozen bodies of other less fortunate native travelers who dared think of Tibet as still their own country. The Chinese, after the recent unrest, were quick to shoot at the slightest suspicion of any traveler who might be a rebel. During their past thirty years of ruthless occupation, Tibetans never had a single moment of peace, nor a safe day's journey. Brave rebels, like Lasker's companions, carried on the fight. They were strong and determined. And unlike the Chinese, well adapted to their land. The Tibetans made the Chinese *pay;* every day!

His Tibetan partners could almost walk up sheer cliffs, and their lungs were like twin-barrel carburetors for oxygen. They were used to heights, and to *fighting.* And that was good, for Lasker sensed that there was a fight waiting up there. In order to free Dorjee—if he found her—they would have to move hard and fast and with devastating efficiency. If they took more than moments to pull off the rescue, they would be discovered. It seemed now that the danger of the ascent was virtually over. Now the only enemy was time. A glance at the low-temp chronometer strapped to his wrist showed Lasker that it was less than a half hour until nightfall. It was Lasker's job to get them into—and out of—the prison with Dorjee before the sun went down. They needed visibility for their risky downward journey. Besides, the temperature dropped rapidly in the winter darkness at this altitude. It would plummet from the current, definitely chilly twenty-below Celsius, to ninety below, in *minutes!*

"Okay, now the last fifty feet! Goggles!" The party adjusted their goggles and climbed out of the ledge. Lasker, mumbling a protective mantra to the Wind-Singer, led the way. Yet the wind didn't favor them. It began to lash at them; the sound of the wind in the flumes of lavic basalt below were creating a low, mournful sound — a humming sound like the plaintive wail of a mountain hermit, or the love song of a lonesome camel. The sound twisted and metamorphosed, became the wind itself. The wind-song was so beautiful that Lasker almost lost his concentration. Only a shout of warning from Tsering below focused him on his goal. "Hold on tight, just a few more feet!"

Minutes later, Lasker's gloved hand closed on the edge of the obsidian fortress's terrace wall. The rock was crumbly up here near the top. Lasker careful swung onto the walkway, then added his weight to the rope to pull the others up onto the terrace. He kept the rope taut until they all had made it safely.

As he coiled the rope about his shoulder, Lasker smiled. He knew that it would be a lot easier and faster going down! And he had no doubts about the equipment stored on the ledge.

"Well, let's go," Lasker whispered, "that abutment up there! Her cell can be reached from the balcony just above it." (One of the things the underground had provided that was most usefully was the plan of the prison!)

With a whoosh, Lasker threw the grapple hook upward. It caught on the abutment almost silently, as the hook was covered with a light coating of silk. An old rebel trick!

Up they climbed like monkeys on a stick. And the intruders swiftly slid onto the prison's narrow second balcony. Then the three invaders ran the fifty feet and around the corner. Lasker, anxious to reach Dorjee's cell, was first in line. And so it was that he ran face-to-face into a guard.

He was a Chinese youth in a red-starred cap and quilted brown parka, and he had his sidearm holstered, as if he was just taking a stroll there. The kid probably hadn't yet reached the age where he had to shave, but he *was* the enemy. He gasped and reached for his pistol. Lasker knew he had to be stopped, yet he hesitated for an instant — because the enemy soldier was so damned innocent looking.

Tsering didn't hesitate. He jabbed the youth in the throat with his dirk, cutting off a shout. Then as the kid gurgled, he grabbed him by his belt and hurled him off the balcony.

Lasker leaned over and watched as the soldier's body fell through a layer of clouds. The one-eyed rebel leader had thrown him far out — so that the kid wouldn't hit any of the jagged rocks near the top of the mountain. Tsering had done the right thing, yet Lasker would never forget the boy's wide-eyed innocent look.

Without a word, they proceeded toward the single, barred window. And as they did so, Lasker noted the wind-worn friezes embossed on the walls of the fortress — ancient, gruesome depictions of obscene rituals: robed figures circling about a great fire coming through the floor of a pillared temple, a huge statue with many eyes and arms and teeth piled high before it — human body parts! This place had been a Bonpo fortress.

Lasker shuddered. The smell of evil seemed to reek here. His highly attuned senses picked up a sickening stench. He sniffed the thin air. Sweat and fear. And there beyond the bars — pain.

His hand wrapped about the window's double bars. No windowpane against the mountain cold!! God, could anyone survive in there at night? He looked inside. Darkness.

Lasker bent his entire E-Kung powered strength to prying the steel bars apart, focusing his chi power, the power of life, into his tortured fingers. Slowly the metal gave.

The bars bent wide enough for a body to pass through.

One by one they dropped down onto an inner windowsill. And Lasker's eyes slowly adjusted to the dark. He dared not use his flashlight, he just waited until he could see . . . Yes!

He saw a shape — a slumped human shape. Jumping down onto a slate floor, Lasker rushed over to the figure that was just a pale smudge in the darkness. He touched cold, naked flesh! He had found Dorjee. He knew that instantly. She was unconscious, chained upright and naked. Her body temperature was way lower than it should be. He touched her temple, found a faint pulse!

Lasker took a chance and lit the small penlight flashlight. She was hanging by her wrists, head bowed over, chained up like a prisoner in a medieval torture chamber. "The bastards," he cursed. In despair that she was chained so cruelly, he began rubbing her wrists, then her ankles. Then he threw all his strength into breaking the chains. With little effort he tore the manacles loose from the wall. And he lay her on his open parka, closed it over her.

"Dorjee! I'm here."

A low moan. She flailed about. Now Lasker was able to draw her arms through the jacket and zip it. A momentary flash of embarrassment that his friends had seen her naked quickly passed. Silly that one can think of such things even in a situation like this.

She was coming around. But her movements were spasmodic. He raised her left eyelid—and saw her almond pupils dilated. Her brown eyes were unfocused. He went to rub her hands again, and she winced in pain. And that's when Lasker found out that Dorjee's left index finger was missing.

"The bastards," he groaned. "Oh, what have they done to you!"

"They've mutilated her hand," Tsering said. "The communists do this to get the names of underground members. One finger at a time, with long periods of waiting in between removals. We are lucky there's only one finger gone."

Lasker's anger flared again. "Only *one?*" he gasped, wide-eyed. "Only *one!*"

"Easy," Tsering said. "I am not the enemy. *Time* is the enemy right now. Lift her! Let's go."

Lasker did so, slinging her easily over his shoulders. Dorjee was slight. Only five feet tall, slender of build. And cold, so *cold!*

"I will transmit warmth from my body," Lasker said. He closed his eyes and trembled for a second. And then he felt the *tumo* heat pass from him. "She is warmer now. She will live. But we must hurry!" Lasker had learned heat-transfer from Cheojey Lama. Cheojey was passing on his knowledge at last. The medical lama had been a good teacher, for as Lasker kissed her cheeks, Dorjee's eyes fluttered open. "A dream . . ." she muttered, and then added, "Bart? Is it really you—or another dream?" Her eyes suddenly cleared, pinned in fear, "No!" she gasped. "No, you shouldn't have come! There are traps. There is a camera-eye in the wall!"

Lasker looked where she pointed. A tiny lens. They were surely being observed, at this very moment.

The sounds of booted feet running!

Quickly he put Dorjee down. Lasker and his men flattened themselves against the wall to the side of the single door of steel.

And as the door clanged open, Communist Chinese soldiers poured into the room. They were armed with smg's. The soldiers spun about, and Lasker opened up with his own Uzi, on full automatic.

And something impossible happened. The bullets he fired just slowed up in midair.

And stopped. The bullets just stood there in midair!

"I don't get it—" Then Lasker saw that not only the bullets had frozen in place, but the soldiers, as well. And his friends, too, were stiff as the Communist soldiers. What was happening? He looked around the cell. Funny, Lasker hadn't noticed those wall friezes before. Nightmarish Bonpo figures, carved on the wall. Robed figures in deep, raised relief, shadowed in the harsh light of the soldiers's flashlights. Stone faces that grimaced. The ancient carvings seemed to move, seemed to shake and wobble, as if animated. Lasker's mind reeled, trying to understand.

And then one of the stone figures detached from the wall and came toward Lasker. All the other humans were as dead, but the stone-wall figures were *alive*.

Chapter Five

A foul smell—like a gas stove with its pilot light out—permeated the cell. Lasker saw smoke. No, not smoke. There was a green, creeping miasma in the cold air itself, issuing from the walls. A strange unworldly tenuous essence flickering with green. The evil power of the Bonpo, Lasker's eternal enemies! He had seen that sudden glow in the air and smelled that horrid fetid smell before. It was the result of intense manifestations of the power of the Bonpo Priest-magicians.

Standing before him, smiling under the shadow of his cowled sea-green robe, was the emaciated corpse-like face that Lasker dreaded to see. It was Zompahlok, supreme head of the evil minions of Yamantalai, God of Destruction.

This fight would be beyond human-to-human—it was a fight against a supernatural force.

The undead man-thing uttered these words: "You are wondering what has happened in this cell. You are amazed, are you not, that everyone is standing still?" The high priest of evil seemed to float slowly across the stone floor, until he was next to a Chinese soldier, the one who was facing the bullets standing in midair. The Chinese wore an expression of fear on his immobile face. Zompahlok touched his skeletal hand to the soldier's neck. The neck caved in, sending a fine spray of powdered skin and cartilage out into the air. The powdery substance stayed where it was, once Zompahlok let go. But the man's neck was half torn apart. Its carotid artery spewed a slowly rising ooze of red blood. An immensely slow red flood.

"Time and space are suspended for these petty creatures, Lasker. But not for us. We Bonpo have use of you. You know, of course, to what I refer."

"You want me to become Raspahloh, your champion," Lasker replied grimly. "You wish to summon to power the other being within me, and to extinguish my personality."

"Quite so," the cat-eyed priest intoned. "Well put."

"You haven't the power to do that," Lasker threatened.

"If you are weakened a bit," Zompahlok said, waving a hand at the figures of stone on the wall-frieze, "it can be done."

And with those words, several garish figures in the wall carvings came forward. Seven Bonpo assassins — including the Bonpo fighting master who had trained Lasker, Phunstok — emerged from the wall. Phunstok took the lead. He was even more formidable and ready-looking then the last time Lasker had faced him.

Why shouldn't this squat and muscular bare-to-the-waist martial artist be ready for the fray? After all, Lasker thought ruefully, the Bonpo assassins were constantly maintained in their youthful strength by occult methods. The process of stealing life from living sacrifices that kept them alive for centuries! A Bonpo assassin was easily more than a match for a mere mortal. They had many E-Kung fighting skills. But beyond that, Bonpo assassins had the advantage of being *unkillable*. BECAUSE THEY WERE ALREADY DEAD!

Lasker bent into a crouch. "So you would challenge me, Phunstok?" He faced off, swinging his mantram-covered sword before the seven magic soldiers. An Uzi was useless against the undead.

The fight now was his alone, Lasker realized. If he failed, Dorjee and the others would die, and by his own hands. If he was transformed into Raspahloh, they would be the first kills.

Lasker pushed forward and drove his specially empowered sword straight at the neck of Phunstok. The blade suddenly just stopped in midair, as if it had hit a wall. It was held there by a green ray. Lasker tried to pull it back, but it was useless. The blade had met a green blast of energy from a glowing crystal skull Zompahlok suddenly held up. The occult blast passed down the blade to the hilt of the sword, and Lasker had to let it go or it would have set aflame his flesh. The sword clattered to the stone floor.

Lasker's arm was numb, still, he reached to retrieve the blade.

"I wouldn't try that," Zompahlok said. Foolishly, Lasker's eyes moved toward the sorcerer when he spoke. Thus, the rays from the skull caught him again. And drew him in. Lasker had the sword-of-power and a special eye-amulet of protection to resist the expected attack of the Bonpo. But this new thing, this crystal skull, and its rays were too strong!

Lasker gave up the attempt at retrieving the sword, and instead grabbed at his "blue eye of Yeshe Tsogyal" amulet. He pulled it from his shirt and held it out. The amulet glowed with power. Its cool blue rays started to force back the green skull-rays. "Get close to Dorjee," he cried out, seeing his friends again moving.

The rebels did so, as a shield of adamantine blue light washed out from the Yeshe Tsogyal amulet, sealing them off from the thrust of the Bonpo ray. They were safe for now—the fight now was to see if they would remain so.

Phunstok rushed Lasker, and the American brought his blade up. Each slashing, expert sword-blow by the Bonpo assassin was parried, and returned.

"Lasker," Phunstok said, backing off, "you have learned much since I taught you. You are quite excellent."

"I'm a quick learner, Phunstok. And you'd best leave here now. My Buddhist masters have taught me some tricks you don't know!"

"Leave him to *my* power, then," Zompahlok ordered the assassin. Zompalok's green slit cat's eyes flickered at Lasker, like coals of green hellfire. He reached out against the blue light again, his skeletal left hand holding high the skull. The green glow flickered in the eye sockets of the skull, hypnotically powerful.

"Ah, do you not ever learn, Lasker? Raspahloh-within-you is the greater part of you. Wither and die, wither and die," he intoned slowly, "wither and die, Lasker . . ."

The words made Lasker's head reel. He was so tired, so tired . . . As he weakened, his blue power-field faded. And the skull's empty eye sockets started glowing even more brilliantly. Its spiraling green rays shot out at Lasker, hitting his eyes, sending a bolt of numbing pain up into his brain. And empowered his monster within. An alien snarl curled out from Lasker's lips. Not his snarl, but Raspahloh's.

Zompahlok laughed. "The petty powers of this world are nothing against our limitless power, derived from the lower realm! Raspahloh will take over your mortal body, Lasker. He will be our champion again. Raspahlo, come join us!"

The skull's glowing eyes held Lasker. Behind him, Tsering shouted, "What's the matter? Why do you stand there? What is happening?" To Lasker, the words sounded like the pounding of heavy surf on a seawall, going slower and slower, like an unplugged record.

"No!" Lasker shook his head, twisting his eyes away from the green rays. "No, I will not surrender to evil; *never!*"

But the skull's glowing eyes would not let go. Lasker felt a welling up of a vile blackness inside him. It was like a rapidly advancing, cancerous growth. It was strong, burning, moving into his arms and legs like molten lead.

"That's the way, Raspahloh," Zompahlok encouraged. "Yes, this is the time! Raspahloh claims your body, Lasker. He seeks only what is rightfully his. Don't you see, Lasker? You must give it up! You do not die, Lasker. You will live through him, as our mightiest warrior. Come forth, Raspahloh, join us. No more pain, Lasker. Obey me! You will go away . . . go away . . . go away."

Lasker fell to the stone tiles, and then his possessed body swiftly rose again, looking somewhat different. He crouched, and drool issued from his twisted lips, lips that pulled away to reveal his snarling teeth.

"Kill, Raspahloh," Zompahlok ordered. "Kill our enemies Dorjee, Rinchen, and Tsering. Do it now!"

As the being that had been Lasker wavered, uncertain, Zompahlok came forward, holding the skull up. "Do it! Do it!"

Tsering, immobilized, kept shouting in Lasker's ear, "Come out of it Bart—OM MANI PADME HUM! Say the mantra of protection!"

"Not Lasker," Tsering's friend snapped. "I am Raspahloh!"

The fight was lost. Lasker had withered under the power of Zompahlok's arcane weapon. Raspahloh was taking over for good. And that meant that he would turn as an enemy on the rebels and Dorjee, and he was fully prepared to follow the sorcerer's command to kill.

In the swirling green rays Lasker was powerless.

"OM MANI PADME HUM! OM MANI PADME HUM!" It was a different voice behind him; softer, weaker, yet full of the power of love. Dorjee's voice. She had sat up and started to recite the protection mantram. The ancient creature that had seized Lasker's body from within began to twitch, to convulse. Dorjee's voice crept into every cell of him, reawakening what there was left of Bart Lasker.

With a scream of ultimate defiance, Lasker tried one last time for recontrol of his body. Tremors shot through his shared muscles; his embattled mind reeled with a feverish nausea.

And he regained himself, if only briefly.

Lasker knew he could only maintain control for seconds, and with more chi-power than ever, he hit the Bonpo assassin Phunstok who was blocking his way square in the jaw, and, screaming rage, Lasker advanced on Zompahlok.

Zompahlok backed off, the skull's glow weakening. He shook his head in disbelief. The tide of battle had changed!

As Lasker pressed forward, a bolt of blue power leapt out from the eye-amulet. It hit the cowl-robed maniac. Zompahlok fell further back.

Once again his Yeshe Tsogyal eye-amulet glowed with blue power. Lasker had regained himself; but could he hold out? Already the green rays were building against him. He shouted, "Tsering! I don't know if I can keep this up! Take Dorjee! Escape while there is still time!"

"No," she pleaded, "I can't leave you!"

"Do it!" Lasker cried out.

The sorcerer from the Hidden Realm again raised the skull. And this time, the green energy smashed at and beat back the blue stream of light until it extinguished the power of Lasker's amulet.

All was lost!

Chapter Six

As Lasker's knees buckled, suddenly the Lake-naga's words from the *prasena*—words that had seemed to make no sense—came flooding into his mind: "When the wall moves, and all is lost, intensify the blueness with the arrowhead."

He had no idea what that might mean! There were two amulets hanging from cords about his neck. One was the fading Yeshe Tsogyal blue eye; the other an old souvenir, the age-blackened arrowhead-shaped sky-object he had acquired in Tibet long ago. The Yseshe Tsogyal eye was losing power. But if he was right about the meaning of the mysterious words of the lake-naga, there was yet a chance!

He held up the arrowhead-shaped sky-object in front of the other amulet. For a second, things were worse. He had cut off the blue rays. And then . . . a burst of white light five times the magnitude of the blue energy issued forth. Incredibly, the sky-object was acting as a focusing lens! Lasker, his hope renewed, found that he could direct the focused beam by moving the sky-object.

The Bonpo sorcerer-supreme was caught in the intense white rays and forced back. Slowly Zompahlok and his minions, screaming curses, had to admit defeat. They backed off until they remerged with the wall carvings.

It was over! Lasker stood for a moment in stunned silence. A greenish mist still floated through the cold cell. What the hell should he do now? His friends and the Communist soldiers still stood in freeze-frame positions all over the cell. How could he unfreeze the Tibetans?

The question became a moot one. The soldiers standing around like mannequins in a bizarre store display started to move! Ever so slowly, removed from the Bonpo energy, they were coming back to regular speed. Lasker acted quickly, and without mercy. He slashed down the Communists with his blade. Powdery molecules of their bodies floated about, and became raw blood and guts. Their slow, drawn-out screams were chilling all the way to Lasker's bones!

Just as he smote down the last one, he saw Tsering's arms move, then Rinchen stirred. His friends had unfrozen, awakening to see a mass of gory bodies sprawled about, with Lasker standing there looking pallid, holding his bloodied sword.

Rinchen did a rapid full circle with his sword up, bending low. He found no standing target for his blade. "What's happened? By the great gods, Lasker! Did you kill all these soldiers?" Rinchen gave a salute with the hilt of his sword to his bloodstained parka. "You are very much the Mystic Rebel! I have been in battle beside you before. You were brave and fast, but never have I seen such—"

"No time for praise," Lasker retorted. "It was not so brave an act! But never mind what happened. Help me destroy the Bonpo wall carvings! Cut them, smash them quickly. Use your blade!"

"But—"

"Just do it, Rinchen. They're interdimensional travelers! The walls came alive!"

"Huh?"

Lasker simplified. "Dammit. They're *spooks,* Rinchen. They came out of the wall! The Bonpo were here, remember? If you don't help me carve up the walls, they will come back!"

Tsering was already at work, having understood. Lasker's explanation about spooks got Rinchen's full attention on the matter as well. Though brave against human enemies, the Tibetan seven-footer hated and feared ghosts and all supernatural things beyond measure.

In a matter of moments they had scarred the walls—particularly the grinning stone face of Zompahlok, who was depicted holding the strange power-skull. Lasker's chi-powered fist made powdery dents where the faces of his primal enemy leered out. And his sword slashed gouges in the stone skull.

"That's enough," he said. Lasker had been going full tilt and now he felt utterly drained, and started to sag on his legs. Tsering's mighty-thewed arms grabbed him, steadying him. "Are you all right, Bart?"

"Yes," he winced, standing somewhat unsteadily. The victory was sweet, but there was no time for celebration. "I almost got transformed in to Raspahloh," he said, feeling a bit more explanation was called for. "Only the amulets, acting in concert, saved the day."

Tsering nodded. "I thought as much. The magic of the Bonpo is stronger every time we confront them! We were prepared, aware they would spring a trap. We had the amulet, the power-sword, and yet . . ."

Lasker nodded. "Zompahlok had a new instrument of power, a crystal skull filled with all the power of green hellfire!"

"Skull? Yes," Tsering remembered, "I *did* see it!" The rebel chief added, "All the more reason to pick Dorjee up and leave this place!"

At that instant a low moan came from Dorjee. Lasker rushed to her side. For a moment, because the parka wrapped about her was splashed with blood, he feared she might be wounded. But it was the blood of a soldier lying nearby. He kissed her lips and she moaned softly. She seemed to be in a daze.

"Can you lift her or shall I?" Rinchen asked, kneeling alongside. "We have to go!"

Lasker elbowed him away and drew himself up. He took several deep breaths. Lasker's recuperative powers were enormous. "Its okay, I can carry her," Lasker said. "Let's get out of here." Lasker quickly stripped off a small soldier's boots and pants and placed them on Dorjee.

Tsering climbed up on the windowsill and Lasker handed Dorjee up to the one-eyed rebel. Tsering took her arms and Lasker her legs, and they drew her through the opening in the bars, with Rinchen covering their retreat, on the alert with his massive sword.

The rescuers were rapidly over the terrace ledge and they began rappeling down the rope in the purple twilight. Lasker had Dorjee over his shoulder. She wasn't heavy, just cumbersome. In the last-light flickers of the red sun, Tsering's copper-coin false eye flashed like a ruby. The silent descent to Lasker was like the culmination of a dream-fantasy; the stars were erupting into brilliance above them in the wine-dark sky. Below them was only inky blackness, and occasional clouds. It was as if they were climbing out into a cloud-streaked otherworld starfield. A place where man had no place being.

As they descended, Chinese Communist troops came rushing from the far right and left along the balcony above. Tsering, the last to descend, emptied his Uzi at them and threw it away. They let the rope burn through their grips to increase their descent speed. In a matter of a few more seconds, they had reached the inset of the ledge. Just as they squeezed into the shelter, their rope fell, cut in half by those above. The Chinese troops then poured down smg fire. Bullets chipped inches from their feet. And the freedom fighters retreated into the darkness. Lasker knew they would be pinned down until a group of soldiers could descend to finish them off with grenades. But they weren't going to wait around for that.

Their means of swift descent was at hand. A wild and reckless method of escape. Inside the package Lasker had brought up by pulley rope were three hang-gliders, broken down into sections. They were specially reinforced for the tremendous strains that would be undertaken. His own wide-design for high altitudes.

"Quickly now!" Lasker implored. In the starlight they found and began tearing open the canvas bag.

Tsering took out the titanium strut-poles and snapped them together in well-practiced fashion. This was done while Rinchen and Lasker unrolled the sets of dull red, yellow, and blue nylon super-strength wings. They all worked furiously, squinting as rock chipped by bullets flew by every which way. Soon they had attached and secured the nylon wings to the poles, creating three wing-winged hang gliders. The tips of the wings almost hung out into the gunfire. The gliders would be chewed up in seconds by bullets if they played their cards wrong, Lasker knew.

One glider was larger than the others—a two-passenger job. As bullets whizzed by, Lasker strapped Dorjee into place in the sling of the larger glider. He stood in a crouch and lifted the wings up, gripped the control bar. He winked to the side at Rinchen and Tsering, who were just as ready. "When that next cloud sweeps by, obscuring us, then we go."

Lasker stared out at the impossible starfields. They were leaving the mountain much later than he had planned. To think that he would step off that ledge into empty darkness made his heart wobble. But there was no choice. No alternatives.

The faint last rays of sun had winked out on the ice peaks of the jagged western horizon. It was already bitter cold and Lasker had given Dorjee his parka. Damn! He should have grabbed a Chinese soldier's parka. There was no replanning now, no going back. Perhaps he'd need Cheojey's frostbite remedies when—if!—they made it down. It was time to go. Where was that cloud? They needed a cloud!

Rinchen and Tsering, Lasker knew, were bold and brave fighters, but to fly from up here, that was asking a lot! Lasker had given them each one hang-glide lesson, on a gentle slope miles away. Rinchen he worried most about—his extra weight, his dislike of flying, even in a 747! Rinchen was reluctant to even sit in an airplane. But the man could guts out anything, Lasker had seen that time and time again.

Finally a black cloud swirled by, just as the shouting above became closer. Communist climbers were mere feet above, descending their way. *"Now,"* Lasker yelled. And he rushed along the ledge and leapt out into the dark nothingness.

There was a violent down draft that made him unable to keep level. He accelerated downward, the hang glider rocking wildly. The only thing to do was go with the downdraft, build up speed, and hope for a side wind to climb upon—before it was too late!

In the vastness of a snowbound-ruined Buddhist monastery, a place that the Communist occupiers of Tibet thought devoid of all life, there lived the Singer. His name was Hsu Fun Kuo, and he was 131 years old. The mountain his collapsed retreat stood upon was miles to the north of the Widow's Claw Peak, yet he saw all that happened there. He had tracked the progress of the three brave souls who had assaulted that lofty evil and had rescued a prisoner held by the ignorant ones. And the Singer had taken pity. Now, in his mind's eyes—his only useful eye, for he had been blind for the past fifty years—Hsu Fun Kuo comprehended that the rescuers on the Widow's Claw were attempting to soar to freedom, soar like the eagle on the exhausted wind. He knew that they were failing.

Their puny cloth wings were not supported by air. The brave climbers would die in seconds. Hsu Fun Kuo's heart went out to them. Why should they die?

So the ragged ancient Singer sang out a long, low-toned note, a plaintive request to the cold mountain winds that knew him so well. And Hsu Fun Kuo began twisting his only possession, a double-hammered Tsaka drum, in his gnarled left hand, to accompany the sorrowful note. His tremulous voice echoed down the stony corridor between the mountains. He sang the lament to the north wind, a wind that he honored all winter long each year, by his mere presence. He sang: "HA ZODUN DEKKO DEKKO HNNN . . . (LIFE IS A SADNESS); ZRI ZAHHO DJINNN HUTTA HRI . . . (I BESEECH THE WIND TO ACT); O-AH HO TRINNN SOKA ZOI . . . (AND PROTECT THE BRAVE ONES)."

The song that he sang was beautiful and sad. As sad as the wail of a Yeti, the Abominable Snowman, upon the death of an infant of its kind; as sad as the cry of despair of a disciple who had lost his master after a lifetime of the master's teaching the way to ultimate liberation. It was such a sonorous, beautiful lament that the elements could not resist. The wind that had gone north at sunset soon was feeling the emotions the song held. And was attracted to it, and moved toward the lament. The Singer's song of lamentation vibrated along the snowy slopes of the pristine ice mountains and they, too, responded. They shed tears of snow-dust.

The clouds driven by the returning north wind rippled in swirling patterns. And the voice of the Singer was joined by the voice of the north wind. It was a fierce icy blast of wind that howled as it rolled down the mountain valleys, wind that sent gravel and small rocks flying off the slopes. Cascading swirls of ice and snow blew from the peaks. The howl became a scream.

And the north wind hurled itself around peak after peak, heading for the Widow's Claw with typhoon force, answering the request of the Singer.

Lasker saw the stars blotted out. The wind was coming in a sudden cloudbank. It hit his plummeting hang-glider like a black fist, and it was a fantastic roiling mass of power. The wind caught the wings just as he plummeted to within a hundred feet of jagged rocks and death. The wind tore at the fabric of his hang glider with such force that he almost lost the grip he needed. Lasker had to twist the metal bar as hard as he could, take advantage of this sudden blast of icy north wind, without totally losing control.

As the wind howled an eerie cry, he managed to stop his descent. The terrible acceleration downward at last over, Lasker soared at hundreds of miles per hour up into the sky, looking for other wings silhouetted upon the starfields.

There! Two silhouettes — Rinchen and Tsering, off to the west. The miracle wind had saved them, too.

For a second Lasker felt the exhilaration of the uncanny salvation. And then he feared it. What force of immense power was operating here? Above the rip of the wind he thought he heard something like a human voice, a beautiful, awesomely sorrowful voice, filled with tears. A wail . . . sad but beautiful beyond measure! This could not be a Bonpo device, it was the act of a great saint, perhaps the one the Lake-naga had mentioned.

That brief soaring ecstasy, listening to the sound of The Singer, was cut short as the thud of heavy caliber antiaircraft weapons being fired from the prison terrace behind Lasker punctured the night. Lasker rolled the hang-glider, trying to keep it soaring up out of range. At the same time his erratic movements made it hard to get a bead on him.

The Chinese were good shots! A line of holes appeared in the left wing of the hang-glider. But the material didn't tear. Lasker leaned hard right and dove, flying into another cloud bank. Just as he did so, he caught a glimpse of Tsering and Rinchen. Their gliders soared some hundred yards behind. And they were bobbing wildly. Were they being hit? The cloud shot between the others and Lasker's kite. The gunfire faded. Lasker was soon miles away.

Now, in the swift roar of flight, in the bitter cold wind, Dorjee moaned. She had evidently awakened in the icy cold blast of thin air. Now, her features cast in starlight brighter than any at sea level, she opened her eyes and looked at him and smiled. And then she looked down and closed her eyes again. "Dreaming," she muttered. "This is a dream."

"No," he shouted over the wind. "We are in the air. Escaping by hang-glider. You're free, my love." He tried to get a fix on where they flew—was that twin peak to the west Kitchunjunga?

"No," she smiled as if drugged. "It is just a dream! A dream that I am a great red bird. That I can—"

He saw her head jerk back, her eyes widen as she

again peered down at the snowy foothills below. And Dorjee shouted, "Oh my Lord, it *is* real." And only then was she terrified.

Lasker had no time to comfort her. The hang-glider came out of the cloud, and he saw in horror that they were coming up fast on a cliff face. He shifted his weight, angled to dive violently to the right. The glider, part of its wing torn by the gunfire earlier, was almost out of control. But not quite — the danger of the cliff face streaked past them. They soared on into another snowy pass. Must be miles off course, he realized. Which way? No matter, just keep altitude. If he could stay up, he'd find the way. They'd reach Cheojey. And safety.

Cheojey Lama was worried now. Lasker had said if they were not back by nightfall, he should take the horses and leave. He wouldn't do it. Not yet. He'd give them a few more minutes! Bah, sky-travel! The way of westerners. Better to travel in the mind, or the astral body, than risk life and limb in the air. Yet how else were they to conquer that awesome mountain fortress?

The last rays of the sun blinked out on the tallest peak, and a brief flash of long, fading sunlight streamers, red and blue and yellow, shot up like a beacon of hope. Cheojey smiled. An auspicious sign, if ever there was one. And there was yet another auspicious event: Under the sound of the wind, there was something — a sweet murmur on the icy wind of winter. Sad, and beautiful. Could this be the voice of The Singer? There were rumors from time to time of the wind singing. A song almost beyond human endurance in its beauty, one that all travelers in the mountains longed to hear, and, once having heard, would remember all their lives. Was this the song of the near-mythical being called The Singer of the Winds? Cheojey cocked his ear, listening. Yes! A beautiful lament, powerful and sad. The Singer of legend was indeed raising his voice. Surely he was doing so to help the freedom fighters in their desperate rescue attempt!

Cheojey sat down on a mossy rock and listened. And shortly he wept. A humble man, he wept because he felt that he didn't deserve to hear this beautiful thing. Many greater souls, older souls—even great bodhisattvas—had traversed these remote mountains and never had such a superlative experience!

"By the gods," Lasker exclaimed, "I can't stand much more . . ." His hands even in the thick gloves were so cold he could hardly hold onto the bar! Somehow he had thought the worst would be over if they had flown free of the prison. But it wasn't over. Slowly, relentlessly, he was losing the feeling in his hands, and that meant losing his grip on the bar! With all the determination he could muster—and prayers for Tsering and Rinchen as well—he rocked his wings back and forth, attempting to get a view over the many jagged foothills below, to find the long lake that marked the valley where Cheojey awaited them. It was so damned dark, despite the stars! When would the moon rise?

He had completely lost sight of the others, that was

for sure. Dorjee's voice asked, "Are we all right?"

He managed a smile. "Everything's fine," he said, and again climbed on the wind. When he burst through a layer of black clouds, his eyes were arrested by the dim glow low on the eastern horizon. There was the moon coming up. It would rise soon! And then he saw the glint of ice; the long, frozen lake that marked their destination! "That's it," he shouted. "Dorjee! That's our destination!"

And then he exulted to hear the rebel cry—like a raven's warning. And he twisted his head to see a pair of hang-gliders right behind him! The bastards flew better than he did!

Steady on course, following the moon glow against the purple velvet-backed stars of the Big Dipper. Not far now! He thought that he saw the torch down by the stream leading into the lake. A moving orange dot under white stars! Cheojey had overstayed, against Lasker's orders. He was waiting with the horses. The old dog was waving a torch.

The moment of believing they would make it passed. Lasker had one last, awful realization. The air speed was far too high! As he descended, he saw plainly that the pine-tree-dotted valley was coming up way too rapidly. Why he must be traveling hundreds of miles per hour! No hang-glider, not even his, had been designed for this. Two choices: They'd either tear apart trying to stop, or soar past Cheojey, and perhaps be unable to get back if the wind stayed as forceful as it was now!

The wings of Tsering's high-altitude glider approached him, coming alongside. The shout of the rebel leader was joyous, even playful. Tsering obviously didn't understand the danger. "Race you," the rebel leader yelled.

Lasker didn't know what to respond. It was all *his* fault. They might possibly all die, attempting to land now. They could crash down miles off course, die in minutes in the mountain land's hundred-below-zero weather.

Then all that worry was just words. The awesome wind just stopped, as suddenly as it had started.

Lasker, elated beyond measure, began a long, slow wheel-about toward the waving torch, lowering his speed easily, wobbling the red-winged device to bear down on the torch. He had no doubts at all now. That voice on the wind, so touchingly sad! It surely had been the voice of a high lama, a great power of good, protecting them! They had soared to freedom on more than just luck; they'd had the indulgence of a great one.

A shadow on the starfields! Lasker realized that there were many other winged shapes behind them in the sky. Gargoyle-winged pursuers.

The Bonpo!

Chapter Seven

Lasker moaned. He should have expected it. The Bonpo had not given up! A frenzied horde of them followed, gliding on their black-as-night batwings. Zompahlok had recovered from Lasker's counter-thrusts and was now on the attack again! This time it was in the air that the challenge was given!

Zompahlok's bat-winged legion was a hundred yards behind. It was the corpse-king himself leading a V-shaped formation of twenty or more slavering Bonpo assassins. He cried out epithets as they slowly gained on Lasker! Slung in weblike harnesses, the Bonpo had their hands free. Each had a crossbow, and they were shooting arrows. Those magic arrows burst into flames at their tip when they were placed in the crossbows and fired. Volleys of flaming death.

One set of fiery arrows grazed so close to Lasker's wings that he was afraid the fabric would catch fire, but it didn't. Tsering had to jerk violently to the side to avoid a direct hit, and he did. Lasker's lessons in the use of the hang-glider had worked well on the rebel leader. He worried about Rinchen, though; the strongman was soaring well off to the side. The Bonpo were now veering on their bat wings, spreading out. They weren't aiming to down just Lasker! The other gliders were in danger as well.

Zompahlok was shouting in glee, and for good reason. His forces were just seventy yards behind, then sixty. Gaining fast! Lasker decided instantly to bypass Cheojey, to gain altitude and speed if possible. Even if he and the other aerialists were to meet a cruel fate, no use leading the evil ones to Cheojey.

Now Zompahlok's voice came into Lasker's mind — like a shard of sharp ice: "Let go of the bar. Let go. Don't worry. We will catch you, Raspahloh."

And the icy fingers of a psychic hand closed over his brain. "No, I won't do it," Lasker raged back, shutting off his mind to the demands as best he could. And without the green-ray-sending skull shooting its poison at him, he was able to resist. He climbed on a welcome gust of icy air, and the others of his party rapidly followed suit.

The insidious cold voice from the Twisted World came again into Lasker's mind. This time, it had a subtler request. "Raspahloh: make him drop the girl. With the girl lost, all things are possible. Exert yourself to make him let her go."

That suggestion to Lasker's enemy-within was yet harder to fend off. Lasker was still weak, it seemed, from the first mental assault in the prison. Still, he managed to quell the torrent of evil-power seething up from within. It was as if the different muscles and tendons in his hands strained against one another! But still he didn't let Dorjee drop!

Lasker, his head swirling, kept gaining altitude and

swept north again. And once again he plunged into black, swirling clouds. The stars went out one by one, as if a giant hand was covering them. And then came the lightning! An unusual winter thunderstorm! No wonder the updrafts were so powerful. Huge spinning balls of lightning flashed down like bowling balls of doom, immediately followed by peals of awesome thunder. As if things weren't bad enough! The gliders were not good in such storms. Lasker should have veered off, returned to the south where it was clear. But the Bonpo would pick them off there. He had to persevere.

He caught a glimpse of Dorjee's terrified countenance in the flashes of light. The winds were buffeting them right and left — so hard to keep control. "Hang on, Dorjee, we're not done for yet."

Tsering's glider now came so close they would have collided were it not for Lasker seeing him in a flash of lightning and pulling up. Lasker, for a millisecond, took in the surprised expression on the rebel leader's orange-lit face, then Tsering was lost from view. Rinchen's wings were also visible for an instant. He was lower, and a bit ahead, rocking in heavy rain. Where were the Bonpo?

A set of flaming arrows swept by, and fell into the sodden and turbulent murkiness. *That's where they were!* Lasker grimaced. Looking back, he saw the batwing squad was actually managing well in the storm. The Bonpo were in formation, in a wide V close on one another. Their flaming arrows kept coming, getting closer to target, too. The hordes of hell were gaining, despite the storm winds. Then, with more peals of thunder heralding their arrival, golfball-size

73

hailstones started to pound Lasker. He felt the craft that he flew grow heavier.

Icing up! He could hardly maintain altitude. This wasn't going to work!

Zompahlok's sky-brigade was finally having trouble, too—the incessantly pounding balls of ice were sticking to their bat-wings, shards of ice making them mishappen, unable to cut the air. As Lasker shouted in joy, the leftmost of the deadly Bonpo pursuers—the one dogging Rinchen's tail—veered. His wings were breaking up. The unfortunate Bonpo, shorn of his wings, screamed out a cry as he cartwheeled downward and disappeared in a cloudbank. Then another fell, and another!

The hail was Lasker's friend. And the wind that brought the ice storm once again sang. This time the song was anger, not sadness.

Lasker heard a faint, windblown curse, and saw the bat-wings of Zompahlok turn back below him. The Bonpo leader was breaking away, with his remaining hell-creatures following. Giving up the pursuit. In Lasker's mind came the hissed words, "We are not done yet!"

The storm of ice didn't abate. The freedom fighters, Lasker knew, wouldn't last to taste the victory if this kept up! Even if the ice didn't tear or weigh down his nylon wings, Lasker was being beaten insensible by the hail. Soon he'd pass out.

How far had they come? Which way back to Cheojey? Should he even attempt to return whence he came? He decided to follow the wind to the left. Then, as he came out of a cloud, he saw the waving lantern, and it was dead ahead. The storm had blown

Lasker's glider where he had come from!

"There!" Lasker exclaimed to Dorjee, not knowing if she could hear." There is salvation!"

Lasker cut speed by twisting the bar up and doing a full 360-degree vertical loop, hoping the fabric wouldn't tear from the centrifugal force. It didn't. And that maneuver cut the forward speed. He tilted the wing steeply and turned sideways. The others followed, diving for the orange lantern light waving before them. The staccato beat of hail died down.

Now that there was more than a semblance of control, Lasker briefly wondered: was that gleam of torchlight truly Cheojey's signal—or some foul Bonpo trick? Too late to do anything about that danger now!

Lasker came in low and fast. Still, it was a reasonably controlled approach. He could see in the flashes of lightning the silhouetted stallions, rearing up. And the small shape on one horse, waving the light. Yes, it was Cheojey.

As Lasker landed, he twisted to a vertical position and he let his feet hit the frozen turf. He ran as fast as he could, and with each step tried to slow their momentum. Finally the hang-glider tilted to the side and twisted to a halt—breaking up in the process.

"Dorjee!" Lasker cried out, unbinding her from the harness. She managed to raise her head, and in the flashes of skylight, he saw her eyes focus on him under drenched, tousled black hair.

"So *cold*. Have we landed?"

Lasker answered, "Yes. Rather ungainfully, I'm afraid. But any landing's a good landing!" He helped her up and found that she had a few elbow and knee scrapes, but was otherwise uninjured. Stumbling in mud and snow, he helped her rise.

He heard the terrified whine of a set of horses and just then he saw Tsering's wide red wings flash by. "Tsering!" he yelled. "Cut speed. Land!" But he didn't know if Tsering heard him.

The rebel leader was having a tough time with the fierce gusts of wind, but he managed a turn and then came back, low. Lasker watched as he got to within a few feet of the tundra, and then his heart did a flip as his friend's wings collapsed! Tsering dropped fifteen feet — onto the snowy bank. And skidded to just feet from Cheojey's three mounts.

Lasker rushed over, tearing away twisted frame and fabric, and lifted the man's head into the cradle of his arms. "Tsering!" For a second Lasker thought that Tsering would not rise up. But then Tsering responded to his repeated entreaties. "I'm okay. Where's — "

THUD. Rinchen landed against a small, twisted pine tree. The huge man, cursing, struggled to get out of the twisted mess that had been his glider. It had been close, very close, for all of them.

It was all they could do to get up on the frightened horses, but they managed. Somehow they had survived their escape and were all together.

Lasker had never felt so triumphant — and lucky — in his life. "We ride!" Lasker screamed, snapping the reins of his midnight-black mount. Dorjee rode in front of Lasker on his saddle. The lowering clouds enveloped and seemingly ate the lofty peaks.

As they tore up a defile, hoofs sparking on the flintlike rocks of a mountain, there were wild shouts. Cries of hatred and blood-lust just a hundred yards away—in the tree line! It was the battle cry of the Bonpo. Some of them had made it down to a safe landing, it seemed. There they were, their cat-eyes glowing in the near total darkness, amid the gnarled pines.

Lasker gritted his teeth, and bent low into the wind. They couldn't pursue—they had no way to do so.

Or did they? For as the war cries continued, the Bonpo eyes moved rapidly. They were *mounted*. On what? The roar of fierce feline anger answered his unspoken question. The Bonpo came rushing from the copse of trees, riding snow leopards. They had summoned the mountain cats, and rode them. Being light, because they were dry corpses, not men, the Bonpo could be carried easily by the fierce cats. And a snow leopard was fast. Lasker knew the cats could outrun a horse!

Chapter Eight

They temporarily at least had lost the pursuing Bonpo in a twisting maze of avalanche-tumbled boulders.

The ice storm had abated, the clouds had swirled away. The hooves of their steeds flashed sparks on the frosted rocks. They rode for their lives, barely aware that a giant full moon rose, until Lasker saw a familiar profile silhouetted against the moon's face. A pine-covered knoll with the outline of a man's face! He knew he was near the tiny village of Yarang, where Rinchen's uncle had a corral and a drinking house! Which meant that the riders were coming up on Gayarong Pass! The pass contained the home of Lasker's master, the Hermit. Had fate planned it that they would be driven to ride this way? If so, there was just one chance for safety. "Follow me," Lasker yelled, pulling the reins taut and turning his midnight-black steed onto a steep, slaggy defile.

"No!" Rinchen yelled, believing that the American was heading for Yarang, which had been a rebel stronghold. Yarang recently had met the fate of many such places. The town had been demolished by the Communists! Lasker didn't know that that town was destroyed, and that the hills hereabouts were now full of Chinese patrols! "Stop him," Richen yelled. "He is leading us to doom!"

But the lama ahead, and Tsering, too, either did not hear or did not wish to heed Rinchen's entreaties. So there was nothing for the massive freedom fighter to do but follow. And die bravely. Rinchen hoped his death would come by a bullet or a blade from a human enemy, and not from the night-creatures pursuing!

Lasker, with the other horsemen close behind, reached the top of the knoll and peered through the trees down at the town. Or where it should be. He saw no lights. And as the scudding clouds passed from the angry red full moon's face, he beheld blood-dark ruins where buildings had once been. And absolutely nothing where the brew house of Rinchen's uncle had stood. A flashing memory of the roaring fire in the brew house and the sound of hearty voices of rebels bragging and carousing in magnificent drunkenness assaulted him, and then he brought his mind to the emergency at hand.

Whatever had happened to the town, that was not their destination this night! Lasker turned his horse to ride on between the two peaks nearby; maneuvered it swiftly among the massive tumuli of many an avalanche. He headed directly for the Oracle Cave near the leftmost peak, about two-thirds up.

The climb was steep and difficult for a horse. Perhaps, Lasker reasoned, that was why the others lagged behind. Dorjee lay against him, bouncing like a rag doll. She was undoubtedly exhausted. Asleep, or unconscious, he knew not. He felt her warmth against his leather vest. She was alive.

There would be help in the cave, if they could reach it. A long climb lay ahead — and the Bonpo . . . how far back were they? He looked back. Lasker could see far and wide now in the lunarlike moonswept terrain.

No doubt about it: the Bonpo were gone. Perhaps these hills, steeped in the power of the Buddhist saint — recluses since time immemorial had cast a shadow on the Bonpo power, or — the Bonpo had circled ahead!

Lasker continued the climb a bit more slowly. The horse he rode was dripping with sweat, despite the intense cold of the evening. Its mouth was flecked with foam. He didn't want to have it die on him. Not now!

By the time he reached the cave entrance — a jagged crevice in the face of a cliff amongst tumbled boulders — Lasker's companions had been informed by Cheojey of their likely destination. After all, it was Cheojey Lama himself who had first told Lasker of the cave. Lasker felt a surge of warm familiarity here. It was in this cave that Lasker had met up with the mysterious hermit, and had been told that there was no going back to his old existence. Told by the Hermit that he was to forever more be the Mystic Rebel, champion of the light, opposer of the darkness. And told that he must follow an internal star, that no one could really say what Lasker should do except follow that star, wherever it would lead. A lump formed in

Lasker's throat as he approached the cave, a place so close and sacred to his heart.

When they dismounted Lasker whispered, "Don't tether the horses. We will release them to roam free; they are spent in any case. We can't take them inside the cave; the entrance isn't big enough."

The party, without removing the flat saddles and saddle rugs, slapped the horses' hindquarters and sent them rushing down the slope. "Hope and pray they wander far before daylight," Tsering uttered, reflecting the universal sentiment.

"Maybe they will make it back to Uncle Jetsum's village corral," Cheojey encouraged. "They are well trained!"

Then the party, with Lasker carrying Dorjee, made their way into the darkness of the crevice. Their breathing amplified by the closeness of their passage sounded like racing steam engines. They were all near the breaking point.

"I've found it," Lasker whispered. He had been feeling the rocks ahead, going by their familiar undulating texture and his instincts. He had come to a warm draft. "As I hoped, the covering rock has rolled aside — it does so of its own accord at the full moon!"

Lasker heard a short snort of skepticism from Rinchen. But he, like the others, followed Lasker into the warm draft. Lasker held the edge of the roll-rock that served as a door as they entered. Letting the others pass him, he then turned, and with a less-than-gentle pressure, dislodged the door-boulder. He swiftly rolled it back to seal them in.

When the door-rock boomed into place, that didn't sit too well with Rinchen, but he was quieted by

Cheojey. "Can we light a torch?" Tsering asked.

"Not yet," Lasker replied softly. "Light may leak out along the edge of the doorway. Keep walking — it's safe. Trust me."

After that, it was a blind-man's journey, hands holding the garment of the man in front of them, until, finally, the American said, "Okay, now we can find one of the large candles here, and light it. We're far enough from the entrance." The amplified sounds of Tsering's flint being struck, the blowing on the kindling in his hand broke the stillness. Then they beheld the circular chamber of perfectly hewn rock. Dorjee found the large single candle, off to the side.

Tsering transferred his flame to the dry wick, and dropped the kindling. As the candle flame grew, they could see clearly the many primitive red-and-black wall drawings: animals — some of them now extinct, and stick humans depicted throwing spears. Also some blasphemous writings — in Sandskript! The graffiti of a thousand years ago. A spiraling tunnel shaft, constructed for smoke to exit the cave, twisted off in the angular ceiling. But all that was not what caught the rebels' gazes.

"What's that?" Tsering asked, directing their attention to the desk-size smoky blue crystal that stood smack in the middle of the cave. It was octagonal in shape, and pointed at its top.

"That crystal," said Lasker, "is the way that the Hermit will come to us. Or how we will go to him!"

"I don't understand," Tsering replied, mystification in his hushed tones.

"There is no other entrance or exit from this place," Cheojey explained, "except through the crystal."

Rinchen scratched his head. "Why don't we just leave here the same way we came? We can hide here for a day, and then leave."

"Because," Lasker said, "even if the Bonpo don't grab us, the Communist soldiers for a hundred miles have been alerted by now of a breakout at K-5 prison. They have our descriptions. I doubt we can get more than a few miles more. And come daylight, the horses we shooed away will likely be discovered. I don't think the soldiers will find this cave as the hoofprints will be lost on the rocks. But they will know we are in the area."

"Lasker has another reason for coming here," Cheojey added enigmatically. "Even he doesn't yet know what it is."

Rinchen took this in and then plopped down on one of the five dusty red cushions facing the huge smoky quartz crystal. "What do we do? Sleep?"

"No, meditate," Lasker said. "We have to meditate to escape." Rinchen looked surly. He was a man of action.

"Just do as your friend Lasker says," Cheojey stated. "I will help you along, Rinchen. I know you are not much practiced in this method. Just relax your mind, and I will link with you."

They all sat down on the cushions. Lasker was a big amazed that there was the exact number of cusions needed. Always before, when he had entered this Reception Cave, there had only been two cushions. Had someone anticipated their arrival?

There was a brief period of settling into rest, and then the lama spoke. "Close your eyes loosely, not tightly," Cheojey intoned. "And follow your breathing, regularize it, slow it down. I think Lasker will provide us with some surprises, very soon." Then — utter silence prevailed.

In minutes there was a calming in Lasker's mind that came about so swiftly he knew it could only be because of the presence of the old medical lama. Lasker always liked to meditate with Cheojey. The aged lama had a presence of the subtler level of consciousness that could envelop and sooth one's very being!

They were deep into a blissful quietude within a half hour or so. That's when there came a noise, the grinding of the barrier rock at the cave door being dislodged. And then came the hair-raising ululations of hell-beings! The insane, unnerving war cries of the Bonpo sorcerers!

Rinchen's eyes popped open and widened. He was scarcely cognizant of the dim glow from within the crystal. "They have discovered the entrance," the rebel strongman gasped. "We are trapped!"

Chapter Nine

Lasker said, "Sit down, Rinchen. I know it will take them a while to figure out how to move the great rock. Just keep your eyes closed, we must keep meditators. Cheojey, bring him back into the spell—it is beginning to activate the crystal! And that's our only hope."

Rinchen quieted down again, under Cheojey's soft urgings.

The crystal's blue glow could be seen through closed eyelids now, growing brilliant as the noonday sun. Their shared consciousness was resolute. The mediators soon felt as light as balloons filled with helium. "Stand up," Lasker said without uttering a word. The command was inside their collective mind. Telepathy is easier in a state of meditation.

When all had arisen, he began to lead them around the immense glowing crystal, at a quick pace. Lasker wished he could cut this part of the routine of teleportation short, but they *had to* walk about the crystal sixteen times. A hum grew and grew in the still air. It came from everywhere—nowhere.

And then they *floated*. "Hold on," the American cautioned them all, "don't let go of one another's hands. Keep your eyes closed, or we are lost." He squeezed Dorjee's right hand; she squeezed back.

Rolling feelings, like in a banking airplane, the pressure of an ethereal wind—a feeling of flying of into infinite space. And then they felt the earth beneath their feet again. And the cessation of the hum.

"You can open your eyes now," Lasker said. "The Bonpo will never reach us here. We are safe."

Tsering looked about and his eyes were arrested by the sight of an elongated statue: It depicted a seated man, exquisitely wrought out of the living rock of the cave wall. And there was what had to be a three-hundred-carat diamond glinting from the forehead of that serene-faced statue. It was impossible, but they were not in the same cave!

"That," Lasker said, "is the Peaceful Deity statue. And we are in—"

"The Peaceful Deity Cave," Tsering finished in a hushed tone. "Why that's near Shemar Rimpoche's monastery! Hundreds of miles from Gayarong Pass. How on earth did we do this?"

"*Not* on earth," Lasker smiled. "We discorporated our bodies and ignored all time and space constraints, and traveled through the crystal. I could hardly believe it myself, first time I did it."

"A miracle," Rinchen said. "I have been part of a miracle. I must be a very powerful being in my mind, too, not just my body." His barrel chest swelled inside his size fifty-two gray parka.

"Don't flatter yourself," Cheojey admonished. "It

is not your power, nor mine, nor Lasker's that allowed this. It is the power of the Master of the Cave. Without him, we would have left this life. Our body parts would have been piled before the hideous Yamantalai, Lord of the Bonpo sorcerers."

"And where is this Master?"

"We will find him." Without another word, Lasker went over to the statue and disappeared behind it.

"Bart! Don't leave me behind," Dorjee pleaded.

"I'm not leaving anyone. I'm finding us some tea!" Lasker quickly found the wood-fired stove and heated the hot, buttered yak tea that Tibet was famous for. They sat against the warmstone walls and drank from cracked cups. Cups of an ancient funnel-shaped design.

"Who left us this tea? Does the Master look like that statue? I hope not!" Rinchen was full of questions.

Lasker replied, "No, that is the figure of the god of the Cultivators — an ancient race of space aliens." Lasker half-smirked, though it was true!

"Aw, you tell tall tales," the Tibetan strongman complained. He took another sip of his tea.

But then he froze in place. His teacup dropped into his lap, and Rinchen quickly jumped up as the hot tea hit his flesh. There was a new presence in the cave. A huge shadow.

The looming shadow, twelve feet high, was coming from an adjoining chamber. And the scratching on the stone flooring sounded like claws scraping stone.

No one else noticed at first. Then Lasker looked at Rinchen's pallid face, and turned to where the strongman was pointing. He stood up. "Company,"

Lasker said needlessly, for all were on their feet.

As the thing that cast the long shadow wobbled forward, a booming voice echoed in the cave. Some primeval monster's yowling? They all crushed back against the far wall, as the shadow slapped forward, and shouted out, "AHWANTTHCOOSI! COOZIEE, WHOOOORSTHECOOZ?"

"By the Buddha! What is it, Bart? Is it saying something?" Tsering asked. He fumbled for the Uzi he had discarded long ago.

Lasker smiled. And suddenly untensed. For the diminutive figure that was casting the giant shadow had now stepped into the bright light and was limned there, between the chambers. And its yowl, less distorted now, seemed much like words. AGain the "thing" spoke, and this time Lasker plainly made out the demand it spoke: "Where's my cookies?"

"*Cookies?*" Tsering asked. "It wants cookies?"

"Put away your swords," Lasker frowned. "It is the Hermit."

From out of the brightly lit passage stepped a scrawny old man with long fingernails, wearing a turquoise-colored robe.

"I thought so! So, it's you, Hermit!"

"*It's you, hermit, it's you, hermit,*" the Hermit mocked, repeating Lasker's words. "Of course it's me. Why state the obvious! Why were you so afraid? Oh! Hee hee. The shadow . . . Listen, Bart Lasker, it is very good to see you. But where are my cookies? You *did* bring cookies? Oreos? Chocolate chip?"

"Who is this demanding old fool," Rinchen snorted, much embarrassed, now, that he had been so frightened. "I will teach him a lesson!" The massive clan sword was drawn in anger.

Lasker raised his hand, "I don't think you understand, Rinchen. This is the Master of the Cave."

"You? You are the Master? This scraggly bearded old Hermit is a master?"

"Yes, I am the Master! And this is the Peaceful Deity cave," the Hermit mocked in a sing song of irritation. "And where are my cookies? You all didn't come empty handed, did you?"

"I'm very sorry," Lasker said. "We didn't expect to be visiting you." He looked down at his boots.

"No cookies? Indeed." The Hermit looked disappointed for a second and then said, "Well, that's life. First noble truth: Disappointment." He peered at Tsering and then Cheojey and finally Dorjee and said, "I think all of us have met once before."

Cheojey was the only one who remembered. "Yes. You were in a rather disheveled state then. We thought you a beggar. Then we saw some of your power—the power to dispel a storm. So it is *you* that has become Bart's master! The wonder of it!"

"Yes, I do remember your stupid reactions to a little dirt! I *was* rather unkempt at the time I first met you all. But that was because I was meditating for a year—without food or water—when you disrupted my reverie. I've cleaned up my act, as the American would say. I wear the robe of the Cultivators now. Made of self-cleaning material. No need for laundry days, hee hee. Oh, now I suppose I should join you all in tea." The Hermit snapped his fingers and a cup of steaming tea appeared in his hand. As soon as this happened, Cheojey prostrated to him, and so did the others. All except Lasker.

The Hermit looked at Lasker and shook his head. "Again it is only my single sole disciple on earth that has the disrespect not to kow-tow. Such are the Americans! Well, you might as well all rise. The tea is getting cold."

Cheojey, as he picked himself up off the rock floor, gave Lasker a sour look. "You don't respect your master?"

"Oh, sure I do," Lasker said. "It's just that I have to be—independent."

"Yes it is true," the Master yawned, gingerly sitting himself down on a cushion. "Now, come on, while we sit and have tea. Explain to me, Lasker—how is it you all came to visit?"

"Hermit, I will. But first could you help Dorjee?"

"Eh?" The Hermit looked again at Dorjee and then blinked rapidly and said, "By the Great Bodhisattva, you're right. Her life-aura is very unbalanced—exposure and an upper respiratory infection and . . . my God, child! You were tortured. You recently lost a finger. Two days ago! Lay her here, on this straw pallet. There is a slight infection of the hand where the finger used to be. I definitely need to do something." He fussed for a while, adding, "Here, let me show you all something. Cheojey, put these on." He handed Cheojey something that looked like cracked aviator's glasses, smoky glass hard to look through.

"What is this for?" Cheojey asked, putting the goggles on loosely.

"They show the 'auric field' better, if your eye for such things is poor. Can you see? It is all pear-shaped instead of being round. Especially near her waist."

Cheojey nodded, took off and passed the glasses to

92

Lasker. He, too, saw what the Hermit meant. In the lenses Lasker observed that Dorjee had a glowing frame of pearl-gray. Lasker drew the Hermit aside, and voiced his greatest fears, "Is she in any danger for her life?"

"Of course not—she'll be fine. Can't restore that finger, though. But I can fix that aura! Cheojey will help me."

Dorjee, overhearing, smiled gamely and said, "I have other fingers."

While the Hermit began to apply a hot poultice to the young woman's other fingers, Cheojey applied moksha-burning to several areas of her back, stimulating the healing channels of the body. Lasker quickly summarized the events of the past day as they worked on her, leaving little out.

When Lasker had finished, the Master-of-the-cave said, "I see! Well, you certainly had to get out of that area of the country the quick way. But don't assume you're safe here. There has been a disturbance in the aura field of the whole Himalayan mountains. The Bonpo have acquired some huge new energy source— probably that is what powers that strange crystal skull you mentioned, Lasker. It won't do for you all to stay here; we must fix you all up, and then get you on your way." He removed the herbal poultice. "There, you'll be better now, soon, Dorjee-la."

Cheojey Lama kept to his work on her back. She seemed to relax, sighed in relief. "Feels warm and wonderful," Dorjee said, as Cheojey finished up.

"She will recover nicely," the Hermit said. "Now,

93

Lama, help me recite the seven-line prayer—to give help to all of these brave men whose bodies and minds are sorely taxed. The chant will align their bodies, and cure their imbalance. You will all sit and relax for a spell and let my tea warm your insides, rebalance your half-frozen energy channels by chanting. You don't want to be sick do you, Lasker?"

Lasker said, "No. And I thank you for your ministrations, Hermit."

They sat and solemnly recited the seven-line prayer. Like most Tibetan chants, it wasn't just a prayer, it was a medicine—a harmony of tones that rebalanced life-energy. In Tibet, there were all-purpose chants, like this one, and then there were highly particular chants—for specific diseases, like cancer. The Cave Master led their song in a surprisingly loud voice, accenting the syllables oddly, drawing up the power of the metal in the earth and placing it in the sounds. This went on for perhaps a half hour. Then the Hermit faded his voice out, and they all followed suit.

"Now, don't you all feel better?" The Hermit raised his bushy white eyebrows.

It was truly remarkable. All felt immensely relieved!

The Hermit nodded. "Well, let me say that you are all most fortunate to come here at this time. I have come upon a great and wonderful discovery! You must see for yourselves."

Lasker frowned. "It's probably very interesting, but we have to leave you. Dorjee is a prison escapee—her picture will be distributed. We must quickly cross the border into India. And like I say, the Bonpo are after us. Only at the palace of His Holiness will we truly find safety."

"Well! You're not going to leave via my front door—the Communists have set up a fortress in this valley," the Hermit responded.

All moaned upon hearing the Hermit's pronouncement.

"But don't despair. There *may* be another way out. That is, if you all will pay attention to what I discovered. It suits your purpose of escape, I think. So come along!" He picked up his hickory-wood walking stick, led them via torchlight through a wall panel door. They went down into the recently discovered secret tunnel, the walls of which were filled with artwork of geometric symbols.

"Look at these inscriptions—Cultivator language! Where does it go?" Cheojey asked, his soft voice echoing in the tunnel's ancient dampness.

"I don't know," admitted the Hermit. "Let's find out."

Chapter Ten

Running his hand along the absolutely smooth cool tunnel-wall Lasker exclaimed, "This is as smooth as glass. How old do you suppose it is?"

"As old as the mountains themselves, I would guess," the Hermit replied. "And not built by earthly beings."

It gave them all a shudder when he said those words, and the way the solemn syllables echoed down the chilly tunnel.

They went along for about another hundred meters, the torch casting eerie shadows. Lasker noticed that his head was significantly closer to the top of the tunnel. A good foot closer. "The diameter of the tunnel is shrinking."

"That's not the only thing happening," Tsering added. "It's getting a bit warmer." He held the torch he carried closer to his mouth and breathed out, *"Haaa!* See? I can't see my breath anymore. It is growing quite warm."

The torchlight was dimming also. "Do you suppose," Lasker asked, "that the air is getting bad as we descend?"

"Shouldn't we go back?" Dorjee asked softly, voicing a feeling they all had. "This doesn't seem to lead out of the cavern. And, if the air is failing, we could suffocate."

Cheojey took a deep breath and held it for a minute and exhaled. "I say the air is good, just a bit stuffy and still. The torch is very old, and dry. That's why it's failing. We would be better off to just use the crystal light, it is enough. Put out the torch, Tsering, and save it for if the crystal fades." They had no idea how long a crystal light would last. This one was one of two that they had been given by Thar-lan in the nunnery of the Lava valley, several years before. The light the tiny device gave off was like that of a small flashlight. Tsering fished it from a pocket and turned it on.

"Let us continue," the Hermit implored.

The utterly featureless tunnel just kept getting steeper and steeper. At last they reached something: a staircase that spiraled down and down. The steps were very wide, and about two feet high.

"Whoever these were made by wasn't human," the Hermit said as he gingerly took the first step. He seemed to have his foot slide out from under him. He steadied himself and cautioned, "Be careful; they're very slippery. As smooth as the walls."

"Who would make a staircase *slippery?*" Dorjee asked.

"The Cultivators," Lasker said, "the space aliens who I told you about. I met several on my quest for the Padmasambhava text. They had suction cups on the end of their fingers. I saw them. Maybe they have suction cups on their toes, too. That would explain the slippery stairs. Good for suction cups."

Rinchen's face twisted up in the dim light. (He was the most skeptical of all the Tibetans Lasker knew of such "fanciful" tales.) And why should he believe Lasker? The Mystic Rebel was probably the only one alive on earth that had actually *seen* a live and breathing Cultivator!

"Bah," the lantern-jawed freedom fighter scoffed, adjusting his sword so it wouldn't clank as he descended every step. "I don't believe in the giants of old. Many illusions occur in the northern mountains. You were the victim of some such."

"Suit yourself. But I'd like you to tell me who makes slippery stairs?"

"Worn down by constant use," the Tibetan strongman offered rather lamely.

"Never mind. Let us keep going!" the Hermit snapped. Heeding the caution of the Hermit to watch their footing, down and down they went. The party of explorers got into a rhythm and were making good time, but toward what? Lasker groaned when he thought about having to retrace their steps back *up!* They must have gone down twenty or thirty stories already.

Then the staircase ended, coming out into a cave so huge that the faint light couldn't reach the far wall. The floor was of triangular tiles. "Which way?"

"I can guess," Cheojey said, and the medical lama started leading them. "The pattern of the floor all seems to be converging. I say we're heading for the center of the room."

"Is that good?" Tsering asked.

"Oh, yes," the medical lama replied, soon adding, "We stop here. We are at the center. Would you please turn the light off?"

Lasker felt Dorjee's hand tighten on his own. Apprehension.

"Why turn the light off?" Tsering asked.

Cheojey replied, "Just do it. You'll see."

Sighing, the rebel leader reluctantly clicked off the light. They all gasped in wonder as a million points of light that had to be starfields came out overhead.

Lasker said, "It looks like we're in — a huge planetarium. What are those thin colored lines — green, red, blue — some sort of markings of constellations?"

Cheojey disagreed. "If they're supposed to be stars, the starfields aren't right. All the stars are all out of place."

"They would be," the Mystic Rebel stated, "if these stars represent the position at the time that the Cultivators came to earth many thousands of years ago."

"Good guess but wrong," the Hermit said. "I say they are representations of ancient starfields around the home planet of the Cultivators. The lines could be trade routes or some such."

Suddenly the medical lama giggled. "I disagree."

"Then what is your sagely wisdom?" Tsering snorted. "Pray tell us."

"Remember when we were in New York City? Was there not a map in the subway of the various transit routes? Use your common sense — why put a planetarium in a tunnel? I say this is some sort of map of the tunnels," Cheojey reasoned. "The brighter colored dots would perhaps represent stations, the lines, various tunnels."

"Good. I like that theory," said the Hermit. "And I will add something. The brighter stars could be stations that are express stations. All around the globe. Haven't you noticed that there are jagged lines, seemingly random shapes. Those shapes are like the shape of the continents! Maybe we are in the entrance to a worldwide subway."

Rinchen said, "I can believe subway trains under big cities, but not under a whole world! You wish to pull my leg."

"Oh, well," the Hermit giggled. "We have made some guesses. Now let us find out. Let's move on."

"Good idea," Lasker said. "The proof is in the pudding."

"Pudding? Where?" Rinchen said, confused.

Tsering put the light back on and Lasker heard his lover heave a big sigh of relief. He would have to keep her close.

They continued to follow the redoubtable lama. When they approached the far wall, they saw that there were shapes in the beam of light. Huge, rounded, metallic shapes, reaching halfway up the sixty-foot height of the domed room. They were of grotesque appearance.

Rinchen's voice shook in awe as he uttered, "What are they? Machines, or skeletons of some fantastic beasts?"

"They look more like huge insects," Dorjee whispered. "Are they dead?" Her hand again squeezed Lasker's tightly, seeking reassurance.

Lasker chuckled. "They aren't alive and never were. Haven't all of you seen giant construction machinery? Tractors and backhoes and the like? I think these are tunnel-construction devices."

"But they don't seem to have wheels," the rebel leader cut in. "Big machines for digging would need wheels and some sort of metal claws. And as far as I can see, these have neither."

"Very observant, but this technology is superior." Lasker stepped forward and ran his hand over one shape. He retracted his fingers, marveling at the fact that there was no dust on them. The machine had been *warm*. And now there was a faint click. As they all jumped back, it started to shudder into life. Flashing series of blue-green lights camoen, and a word was uttered softly in a language none could understand. "WHRROOST!?"

The word was repeated several times as if seeking a response. Then the machine shut off—to their great relief. After a minute, the row of lights went out, too.

"Don't touch anything else," the Hermit admonished.

"What was *that* about?" Rinchen asked.

"I suspect that he activated it," the Hermit said. "The machine said, 'What do you want me to do?' I know something of the Cultivator language. You shouldn't touch anything," the Hermit added. "Think for a moment. These tunnels couldn't have possibly lasted for so many centuries without repairs. And before us is the answer to that mystery. I'll bet these machines are self-operating as well as being able to respond to commands. That would explain the response Lasker just received. Some machine like this is making *repairs!*"

Lasker had Tsering shine the light to the side of the device. "I think that last eyelike structure at its narrow end is some sort of rock-dissolving device—a laser or something. That could be very dangerous," Lasker offered.

"Right!" the Hermit said. "If there's a breach in the tunnel or a collapse—the machines sense it, go out and fix the problem. Very nice! And those *words!*" the Hermit sighed. "So *wonderful* to hear a language so old. I can read the writing of the ancient ones quite well. You know I have studied old documents. But I know very little of speaking their language. It could be fun to learn. I could learn proper pronunciation by asking questions of these machines. I could learn to speak Cultivatorese! For instance, 'WHROOST' must mean 'Ready.' So therefore, the pronunciation of vowels is . . . If only we could stay here a while, I could learn their language."

"Interesting," said Lasker, "and dangerous. Besides, I thought we were all looking for an *exit*. Shall we continue onward?"

"Yes. We should move on," Tsering said grumpily. "I can't wait to get away from these things. Suppose they decide *we* are tunnel obstructions that have to be cleared away?"

With that frightening thought, they hastily spread out and searched along the smooth curving wall by hand for an exit.

"Over here!" Cheojey called out. "There's something like a door." When the search party came to stand alongside the diminutive lama, he manipulated a little knob and a panel slid open. Darkness ahead. Another tunnel.

They proceeded through the triangular-shaped door arch and down at a slant. Soon they started to encounter a wind. And then their breathing became labored. "I don't think it's bad air. It's just that we are so far down, the air pressure will build up. Not too much to bear for human lungs."

"We should go back then," Rinchen said. "I am not a mole!"

"No. Look there," Cheojey exclaimed. "That shape—"

They moved forward. A long cylinder set sideways blocked their path. "The wind and pressure is coming from the long narrow tunnel that this tube points into." There was a hatch on the cylinder, which opened to reveal the interior.

"My God. It has a set of huge seats in it!" Lasker stepped in and sat down. "Hey, this is comfortable! Very soft to the rear end. It's some sort of vehicle, I think."

"Like a subway!" the Hermit volunteered.

"Could be. But there are no rails," Tsering pointed out.

"Maybe it floats up off the stone floor when you press a button or something, you know—magnetically," said the Hermit.

Lasker agreed. "It does look like some sort of pneumatic tube like in a office."

Tsering grunted, "Well for God's sake, let's go back."

"It can't do any harm to sit for a spell," the Hermit said. "Shall we get in with our American friend?"

"Okay," Tsering said, entering the cylinder cautiously. "Just be careful not to touch anything." He was glaring at Rinchen, who was clumsy enough to jostle something with his elbows or big feet.

They sat there, resting. Rinchen removed one boot and was rubbing his sore foot, the odor of which was beginning to waft through the car. Suddenly blue lights started blinking on in what looked like a control panel in front of the cylinder-car, within reach of the Hermit's eager hands. "Shall I press a few buttons?"

"No!" was the reply, spoken in unison by all the others.

The Hermit said, with irritation edging his voice, "Oh, come on! I'm surprised at you all. Especially you, Bart. Aren't you the least bit curious? Didn't you once say to me, 'No guts no glory?'"

Lasker grudgingly agreed that they should let the Hermit experiment. "But if it starts moving, or anything else that seems dangerous, cut if off—immediately." The Hermit gleefully started pressing the buttons from right to left. Nothing happened.

"Now what?" Tsering asked.

"Hmm," the Hermit mused aloud. "I think nothing works because we haven't closed the hatch." He rose from his seat and went over to the glassine canopy and started to tug on it. It didn't budge. "This thing must have a safety cutoff switch. Rinchen, you beefy fellow! Can you lend me a hand?"

That didn't work, either, despite several hernia-force pulls. The Hermit sat back down at the controls, puzzled. Rinchen, wiping sweat from his brow, leaned on the hatch-sill. And there was a whine. And the hatch closed.

"Okay!" said the turquoise-robed adventurer. "Now here goes." The Hermit started his button-pressing again. This time, the tube-car lifted up off the stone floor an inch or two. Then it started to slowly glide

105

forward toward the long circular tunnel that led to who-knows-where. *"Enough,"* Tsering shouted, holding onto his seat with white-knuckled hands. "Stop it."

"How?" The Hermit pressed the same button again, and then several more buttons. An alien voice came on, from some hidden speaker, and said, *"Eknarrr."*

"What's that mean?" Lasker asked the Hermit.

"I think it means something like 'prepare.' "

There was no noise, but the car suddenly accelerated forward, entering the dark tunnel. The second it entered the long tube they heard a low whine. Lasker felt himself crushed back into the cushions. "Oh, God, now you've done it," Lasker grunted as he was pushed back harder and harder. The words seemed to not come forth, but rather were pounded into his tonsils. Lasker felt like he weighed a ton—like an elephant was sitting on his chest. "Holy shit," he exclaimed breathlessly. "This thing really moves!"

Though the words hardly were audible, the Hermit, by some magic of telepathy perhaps, picked up his comment and giggled—or rather, grunted, for the acceleration crushed at him, too.

And that awful acceleration grew and grew. Lasker tried to lift his arm, and managed to do so with great difficulty. His seat was alongside the Hermit's, and he was trying to reach the control panel and hit a button he suspected was the cut-off. The one button the old man didn't seem inclined to press! The button was blue, and the one the Hermit hit to start them off had been red. But Lasker's arm flopped back. Too much pressure of speed! The elephant on his chest seemed to double in weight. Soon, he had difficulty merely breathing. Lasker sincerely hoped that this wouldn't go on too much longer. And a horrible thought entered his mind. The Cultivators had built this subway. Suppose, just suppose that their alien bodies were vastly different from human bodies. Maybe the Cultivators could take triple the acceleration a human could take! If so, they might be dead in another minute or two!

But then the force eased up somewhat. Lasker could turn his head, and he saw that they were still all pretty much all right. Of course the entire party were pinned down, but they were conscious and were breathing.

Cheojey managed to utter, "Look, the tunnel ahead is glowing bright red! I think that we're going into a fire."

"Yes," the Hermit acknowledged. "But not an ordinary fire. We've been descending. This might be the molten rock miles under the earth."

As they were surrounded by the blinding redness, Tsering cried out, "It's getting too hot in here. Can't you find a way to turn us around?"

No reply. The Hermit seemed to have passed out. Heat prostration? Lasker, exerting all his tensed muscles in great effort, reached forward and managed to press the blue button. But all that happened was some sort of soft music came on. Strange alien sounds, like bubbles bursting. Pleasant, but not what he wanted!

The heat built and built, to the point where it was just at the level of burning them. Then there was a beep-sound, and some sort of blowers kicked on. The temperature quickly steadied, soon becoming a very comfortable level. The Hermit moaned and opened his eyes. "Ah," he smiled, "nice and cool."

Lasker was amazed, and thankful for the air-conditioning. Maybe the system was a bit sluggish after all these centuries. The bright red glow continued to flash by, almost liquid-looking, outside the glassine hatch.

"Evidently," the Hermit commented, "we *are* going through an area of molten rock. This is fantastic. The tube-train must be made of something indestructible. This is *fun!*"

If thoughts could murder, the Hermit would have died.

After ten more minutes of speeding through the red glow, the brightness faded. They were plunged into darkness, occasionally interrupted by flashes of light — blue, then pink, then green. Lasker saw hints of structure in those colors. They were vast station areas, lined with machinery of incomprehensible purpose. The awesomeness of this subway system hit Lasker then. It must be hundreds if not thousands of miles long! Perhaps it truly was a world-spanning subway!

The acceleration eased more and more. Until there was none at all. Aside from the tiny crystal source, there was no light.

In the hushed silence, Dorjee asked, "Have we stopped?"

"I don't think so," Lasker guessed. "There's still some vibration. I think we've just slowed down. I'm going to get up and look around in the back of the tube-car. Maybe this thing is like a trolley car—controls at both ends."

He was in for a surprise. For when Lasker moved, he floated up off the chair! "What the hell!"

They all stirred in their seats, and those slight movements made them follow Lasker in floating upward.

"Gravity is gone," the Hermit said. "How interesting! Hold on to something. Don't bang your heads."

Dorjee grabbed Lasker's sleeve and he managed to grab a chair arm and pull them down. The others, too, managed to do the same. But not the Hermit. He was playing! He bounced around, pushing himself from one soft wall panel to the next.

Then the train car seemed to do a slow roll-over, as if gravity was reversing. And the Hermit found himself slowly sinking out of the air. He took a seat. "That was fun!"

"What the hell is going on," Rinchen said. "I think I'm going to be *sick!* Are we on a roller coaster? Yes, I am *definitely* going to throw up!"

But the strongman's stomach steadied as the gravity increased and once the floor was the floor again. As a matter of fact, Lasker noted, the acceleration was increasing once more.

"Does this ever end?" Tsering moaned. "We must have gone miles by now."

"More like thousands of miles, I suspect," the Hermit ventured. "We could be anywhere."

The pressure on their chests rose and rose, to the level they had experienced before—a two-elephant-sitting-on-the-chest level!

And as if that wasn't enough, a horrible miasmatic

haze started forming in the very front of the car. It slowly coalesced before their startled eyes into a monster! A hideous pink-thing. A swirling nightmare with a hundred slavering jaws all over its bulbous body. No neck. Eyes like clamshells with purple pupils stuck up on several stalks of flesh. It had six arms, two like human arms, the others more like crustacean appendages, each with claws like a lobster's. Not a welcome guest.

What most attracted Lasker's horrified attention was the right humanlike arm. It held a massive blade of what looked like shimmering rippling steel. The apparition grew totally solid and stood before them waving its weapon. It snarled and drooled like a wounded gorilla. In short, it looked very much like it wanted to do them all harm!

"What the hell is *that?*" Tsering grunted, as he tried and failed to get up.

"Some sort of demon of hell!" Rinchen replied, as he, too, failed to move more than an inch. His hand managed to get to his sword hilt, but was unable to draw it out.

Lasker's mouth was dry as sandpaper. It was up to him. He had to get up and do something before it was too late. Perhaps his E Kung powers would be enough to overcome this awful acceleration. He summoned up all his chi-power. And, muscles trembling and in spasms of near-collapse, Lasker slowly rose.

Rose to face off against what was definitely the deepest, darkest nightmare he had ever encountered.

Chapter Eleven

Lasker willed himself to move—despite the intense acceleration. He moved in front of his terrified, wide-eyed companions to protect them from the beast-with-a-hundred-toothy-mouths. Lasker had little time to wonder how the beast could have stood there with such apparent ease. It was more than strength, perhaps. It had to be some magic.

Lasker forced himself to take one painful step, then the next, forward in the tube-train, focusing all his chi-force to the task. With all the skill and power he could summon, drawing upon his years of practice of E Kung, the secret martial art of the Bonpo sorcerers, he challenged the horrible lobster-thing. "Do not come at me," he uttered, "or if you do, prepare to die."

The creature waved the glistening weapon and wheezed out, "Hvoorsk! Hvoorsk!" And then it stepped forward.

As the lobster-thing raised that strange spatulalike device again, Lasker struck out—a tremendous fist of dynamite aimed at what he guessed was a vulnerable spot—the pairs of eyes on stalks.

And his hand went right through the thing. Lasker took another shot, this time with an E-Kung kick, trying to snap the arm holding the supposed weapon. And again he hit nothing but air. "It—isn't solid," he gasped.

"I thought not," grunted the Hermit, his voice cracking as he spoke against the tremendous g-force. "Now sit down, Lasker. That thing is no threat to us."

"What is it? Do you know?" Lasker backed off and gingerly replaced his aching body in the cushiony seat. As he breathed in oceans of air, relieving the tension of his body, the Hermit gurgled out these words: "That monster . . . not a monster. I . . . think it's the Conductor."

"Hvoorsk? Hvoorsk?" the thing kept asking from its multiple slavering jaws. And it kept waving the heavy-looking device about. Breathing hard, Lasker asked the Hermit, "Conductor? You mean like on a train? Then what is that thing it has? What is it saying?"

"Maybe," the Hermit replied weakly, "it's asking for tickets."

Lasker moaned. "Then what's the stick for?"

"Some sort of . . . punching-the-ticket device. Maybe. I'm not sure. I don't think . . . Cultivators had a monetary system, though . . . Wait a minute, I have figured out the word it is saying. According . . . to the grammar of—"

"Never mind the grammar," Lasker lashed out. "What does it want?"

"I think it's asking where we're going? Hvoorsk means 'What stop do we want to get off?' He'll keep asking until we answer. And until . . . we do, we stay pinned like this, traveling at maximum speed."

"Oh, no," Dorjee panted out. "Please, make the speed stop! I can't . . . take it . . ."

The Hermit grumbled a bit and then shouted out, "Hmvoorm Robeen Rooo!"

The slavering conductor did a sort of salute with its device, which lit up cherry red. The creature faded away, smiling, or something like smiling, with all its mouths. They felt a sharp sideward motion to the left and downward at a steep angle. Still, it was an improvement; the acceleration eased somewhat. "We've entered yet another tunnel," Tsering moaned. "When will this end?"

The Hermit shrugged. "I did my best."

"What did you say?" Lasker asked.

"The only thing I could come up with. Their grammar is so hard that—well, I told it that our destination is the last stop."

Lasker's eyes rolled up. "That's just great! Just great!" he mumbled.

Slowly the whine of speed outside the tube-car lowered in pitch to a hum. Lasker realized that the acceleration was low enough for him to stand easily, and he did so. Everyone leaned out against the windows and watched blue, red, and then green lights pass by. The angle of the floor kept at about a thirty-degree angle.

As the car went slower and slower, Cheojey administered to Dorjee. She was most shaken up by the events of the past minutes, but finger pressure applied to her shoulder meridians soothed her. Soon she was breathing well enough. Lasker was up front in the tube-car, examining the wall. He found a few lenses. "The conductor-thing," he concluded, "was a holographic projection. But if it was just a conductor, why did it look so horrible? Why the ugliness, Hermit?"

"Beauty is in the eyes of the beholder, Lasker," the Hermit replied. "Perhaps the Cultivators preferred some creature from one of their colony planets as servants. They would model a projection on this most-pleasing-of-all smiling creatures. We like stewardesses on airlines to smile at us. Perhaps a hundred smiles is so much the better!"

Rinchen spoke out now, sourness in his tones: "Humph! They can keep that kind of beauty!"

Tsering agreed, "I liked the Pan Am stewardesses much better!"

Outside the tube-car station, lights continued to flash by, but they seemed to be coming slower and slower. An incomprehensible announcement preceded by a bell-tone came over hidden speakers. "Hvoorsklum Sharbarr-Ak!"

"Oh oh," Lasker said, "keep alert. We have just arrived at wherever the last stop is!"

The door raised and they stepped out onto a dimly lit floor. Above them a dome rose some fifty feet or more. It had stars in it, twinkling like inside a planetarium. Another map.

"Well, Hermit? Do you know where we are?"

"Stop bothering the Master," Cheojoy said softly, speaking for the first time in a long while. "Were it not for this man, we would all be lying crushed in our seats."

114

That was true, Lasker had to admit it. They all said they were sorry, except Rinchen.

"Don't mention it," the Hermit said. "Now, look around. See what . . ."

Rinchen had already wandered off a bit, and now he exclaimed, "Over here! There's another tube-car. It's starting to hum!"

As they walked to join the giant freedom fighter, the second car lifted up and started to move down the long tunnel. "It was waiting for who knows how long for an arriving conveyance," said Cheojey. "Now it is automatically leaving, beginning a return trip."

"We should have been on it," Rinchen lamented.

The Hermit frowned. "So would be the words of a lesser man than you, Rinchen. Those are the words of a frightened man. They are beneath you."

Rinchen snorted. They all spread out around the circular room to probe the semi-darkness for an exit.

Lasker soon found a dimly blue-lit ramp that led upward. "This is probably the exit."

"To where?" Rinchen spoke out, voicing all their concerns.

"Who knows, Rinchen my friend," the Hermit replied. "Maybe we're under India somewhere."

Dorjee, touching Lasker's right arm, had hope in her tone when she said, "Coming up in India? That would be nice."

Lasker squeezed her arm reassuringly, but his thoughts were black. They could just as well be under *China*. Communist China.

The Hermit slapped his bony hands together in great eagerness. "Well, my children, since we have no idea where we are, let us get outside and find out!

Nothing ventured, nothing gained."

"Or lost . . ." Lasker muttered under his breath. They strode up the ramp for a long time. Eventually they saw the unmistakable brightness of the sun, shafting onto the ramp through a crack in its ceiling just ahead.

"The surface, at last," Cheojey murmured. "Buddha be praised. All will be well now."

As they hastened to the light, the party entered an area of tumbled rocks. Huge fallen pieces of the masonry of the ramp-tunnel.

"There," Lasker said, "head that way; toward that wide shaft of sunlight. See? Between those pillars standing at an angle. We can get out there!" They soon clambered up among the tumuli of centuries of collapse. And the temperature rose. Tsering unzipped his parka and sniffed the air. "It is damp, and smells like a jungle."

Lasker almost put his hand down on the first sign of life they had encountered. But he drew it away with haste. "There's some nasty-looking spiders around. Watch out."

They went onward toward the alluring sun, clambering up the rocks nearer to the ceiling. They had to stoop a bit to walk. And there they came upon a set of hooks arranged along the wall. Objects were hanging by chains from the hooks. Dull, silvery balls about the size of apples. A dozen or more.

"Shall I?" Lasker said, reaching for one of the chains.

The hermit shrugged. "They're obviously here to be picked up by whoever leaves this place."

Lasker gingerly lifted a chain from its hook. The

116

metallic balls were surprisingly lightweight. He turned first the ball and then its finely crafted chain over in his hands, then passed it around, taking another. Cheojey found that by twisting them slowly, the silver balls could be detached from the chains. Rinchen took one of the mystery devices off a hook, detached the silver ball, and shook it violently up by his ear. "Nothing inside," he ventured. He put the ball in his pocket.

"What are they, Master?" Cheojey asked.

"I'm not sure. But they're here for a reason. I say we take two apiece," the Hermit suggested.

"Why?" Dorjee asked. "If we don't know what they are?"

"Just a hunch."

The hunches of a great Tibetan Cave-master are to be heeded. So they each put a pair of the spheres into their pockets and walked onward.

Chapter Twelve

Though the shaft of sunlight was beaconing brightly, getting to it over the tumbled debris was more difficult and time-consuming than anticipated. And there were the snakes, crawling around on nearly every rock. Huge red hoses with nasty front nozzles. They measured from a few inches long—nice to get in your boots—to over ten feet long. Fortunately, the snakes weren't interested in making their acquaintances. They seemed as eager as the humans to keep out of the way.

After some minutes, Lasker's party were within twenty feet of the brilliant daylight. Lasker could even see a palm frond. Then they heard a familiar whine and a whoosh in the tunnel behind them. The unmistakable sound of one of the floating tube-cars arriving.

They froze in place, listening. Was the car empty? They heard the snap-pop of the tube-car hatch opening. *And then the soft scuffling of human-skin boots.* And there were words being spoken by the booted ones. Harsh, dry tones, spoken low, but nevertheless audible in the echoing passage. Old dialect of Tibetan. "The Bonpo are here," whispered Lasker, incredulous.

"Quick, let's get outside, then," Tsering whispered back.

But when they reached the aperture, they found it narrow. Only Cheojey could easily squeeze through. "Rinchen, Tsering," Lasker said, "lend a hand. Help me move these large boulders over a bit. Cheojey, can you pull the oblong one from out there?"

They strained away, and slowly the boulders shifted outward and to the side. There was enough room for all the rest of them to squeeze through. Rinchen came through last, and his sword clattered against the rocks. The giant fighter got stuck halfway in and half out, and it took a pull on his belt by Lasker to dislodge him. Everyone looked around.

They were at the bottom of a grassy slope; shaped like an old volcanic crater, Lasker thought. Just a few stubby palmettolike growths about. Rinchen bent his ear to the opening they had left, and in an instant said, "The Bonpo are coming this way."

"Let's get up the slope. If there are trees, we can quickly lose them," Tsering encouraged.

When they got halfway up the slope, the Bonpo were already at the exit. Lasker's party were spotted immediately. The chill voice of Zompahlok oozed through the hot tropical air. "Seize them! Leave Lasker to me and the skull."

Lasker took a quick glance back and saw that the Bonpo leader held in his hand the awful skull with green-glowing eye-orbs. They had to get away, fast. He couldn't take another attack by that thing. They all ran, but the Hermit just plopped down on the grass, facing the enemy.

"What the hell are you — " Lasker started to demand.

120

Without saying a word, the Hermit lobbed one of the lightweight metal globes they had taken from the tunnel up in the air. It sailed at the Bonpo, who ducked back into the aperture among the boulders. The sphere hit and rolled a bit and then, as it reached the boulders, there came a tremendous report. An explosion!

The Hermit jumped up and laughed. "As I thought! The spheres are *very* useful!"

When the smoke cleared, the boulders — what was left of them — were all jumbled into the opening. The Bonpo were sealed in — for now.

"Wow," Lasker said. "Good work! Hey, gang, be very careful how you handle those globes!"

The Hermit smiled and crooked a long fingernail at his temple. "Brains," he said, "win out over brawn. And don't worry about setting those things off. The spheres have to be twisted first. I'll show you later. Let's get going."

They scrambled along, Lasker helping Dorjee keep up with them. Soon, they reached the top of the slope. They found they were up on a promontory of mostly bare rock, and before them a jungle spread out. It was on all sides of the circular rim of the crater they had emerged from. There was a smudge of gray beyond the palms, a mountain off in one direction. The sky above was a roiling mass of orange-tinted clouds, giving everything around them a strange unnatural tint. "Maybe that smudgy lump on the horizon is a volcano," Tsering guessed. "An eruption could have caused the odd coloring in the sky. I smell sulphur, too."

"Let's get into the treeline," the Hermit cautioned. "The Bonpo will dig out soon enough."

"Head for the direction of that mountain, or whatever it is," Lasker said, on a sudden impulse.

They ran down the slope and into the safety of the palms. In moments, Lasker noted that the tall palm trees were of an unfamiliar type. They had purple flowers, and large nutlike extrusions all over their limbs. And they were covered with red vines.

"Where the hell are we — India?" asked the Tibetan giant. "Could we have come that far?" No one answered. They moved onward, trying to make distance from the crater. In a matter of moments, they were unsure of their direction. Tsering, the most agile of them, shimmied up a tree. It took a while, for he had to clamber over the tangle of vines, but he shouted down, "We bear right a bit, and we can keep on course. That mountain is definitely a smoking volcano." With that, the one-eyed rebel rapidly descended to rejoin them.

The jungle smelled of rot and of the odd sweetness of an orange orchidlike flower that grew everywhere. There were plenty of monkeys — with rather pointy heads and an orange fur — scrambling among the palms, and some odd birds with long tail feathers of green that made sounds like bluejays. Lasker was much puzzled. For one thing, there were currently no active volcanoes in India. Or China. Or Tibet. Unless an old crater had suddenly erupted. In any case, the trees, the plants, and the birds and monkeys were *wrong!* Where in the hell were they?

"Which way?" asked Rinchen, wiping a green spider with very long legs off his face. He could be casual about it, for they had quickly learned nothing had any intention of biting them — so far. Sort of a gentle jungle. No mosquitoes even. No leeches. Thank heaven for small favors. And yet — it was uncanny. Unnatural.

"Any way is right, Rinchen," the Hermit replied. "Let's make distance from the Bonpo, that's all. I don't like the energy aura around that skull their leader held up."

After about a mile more of zigzagging progress among the roots and twisted fallen branches, they took a breather, sitting down on the rocks in a small clearing. The sounds of the jungle-jaybirds and the chatter of monkeys was incessant now. That noise, plus the steamy temperature, made Lasker sure they had traveled all the way to some remote, southern Indian area he was unfamiliar with. A fantastic journey! He voiced this theory aloud, ending with the words, "What part of India do you think this is, Cheojey? You're the geography-buff of all of us."

"Not India," Cheojey Lama said firmly. "Look, I have been gathering the foliage, tasting it for its medicinal qualities. No familiar tastes. And in Tibet we use many Indian herbs and plants! Also, I saw some very odd carvings on the rocks where we came out. They were an angular, highly stylized writing. And a picture of a snake with three heads and small legs."

"That's right," Lasker said, remembering he, too, had seen the carvings for a brief second as they scrambled out of the tunnel.

The lama tore a tiny flower up from the grass around them and looked at it closely. He handed it around. "This is some sort of miniature purple fuscia. These I know. They only grow in Tibet, as far as I know."

"Ha!" Rinchen said triumphantly. "All is explained. There are a million valleys in Tibet, some of them tropical, heated by natural hot springs even in winter.

We have not gone so far in that damned subway as you think!"

Lasker looked up into the trees, and saw that among the monkeys sat a white cockatoo. "That's a South American bird," Lasker said. "We could be in Peru. There are fuscias in Peru, Cheojey."

"What? Where is Peru?" Tsering asked. When Lasker told him, the rebel chieftain scoffed, "That's impossible. We are, as Rinchen stated, in some hot valley in the mountains of Tibet. That's all." He seemed very uncomfortable with the idea that they had traveled thousands of miles. Dorjee chimed in as well, favoring the valley explanation. And someone coughed an interruption.

"I think you're all wrong," the Hermit said. "This isn't Peru, nor India, nor Tibet. I don't think we are in any place on earth!"

"What?" Lasker exclaimed. "That's impossible. You think we went by subway into outer space?"

Rinchen laughed. "Even I know that you don't reach outer space in a subway."

"Yes," the Hermit said solemnly. "Remember that weightlessness. We rocketed out into space. We're on the moon or someplace even farther."

Tsering laughed. "And what about the light in the sky? Does this imaginary other world have a sun and clouds like the earth?"

"Have you noticed," the Hermit said in ominous tones, "that in the hours since we left the tunnel, the sun hasn't moved one iota? We are on a planet where the days are perhaps weeks long!"

"The sun will soon set," frowned Rinchen. "The clouds play tricks with the light. That is all." That seemed to be the final word, for now. They got back up, and after Tsering again surveyed the way from a tall palm tree, they headed toward the volcano once more.

"I wish the hell we'd find some water. It's awfully muggy," Lasker said after a time. "Cheojey—can you find some vegetation we can derive moisture from?"

"I've been looking as we travel," the lama said. "No luck so far."

The next time Tsering went up a tree, he reported that the volcano was considerably closer, and partly covered by mists.

"There's bound to be water on such a slope," Cheojey said. "But we should come at it from another side. They might have decided we would go this way. And be waiting for us."

They walked more slowly now. Thirst dogged their steps. The sun remained obscured by the clouds, but Lasker was sure now that the Hermit was correct about one thing: The sun hadn't moved one inch away from its vertical position. His watch said 10:10 PM.

Dorjee stumbled on a root, but Lasker caught her. "Are you okay?"

Her doe eyes looked up at his craggy, tanned face with great warmth and courage. "I'm fine." Then her eyes started to roll upward. Lasker had to catch her as she sagged down. "So tired . . ." she muttered. "Can we rest a little . . . just a little?"

"Maybe we can all use some rest," Cheojey said as Lasker put his parka, which he had been carrying, not wearing, under her head. "After all, many hours must have gone by since we eluded the Bonpo. I can't understand why it's still light out!" He didn't show the others his watch. It *had to be* broken!

125

The Hermit gave him a knowing look. "I told you, the sun will scarcely move. We are someplace else than earth."

"Well, we still can sleep, wherever we are." Lasker glanced with worried eyes up at the still-orange, still-roiling cloud cover. *Could it be?*

Rinchen yawned and lay down, and as he did so, he groused, dry-lipped, "I shall not sleep well. I hoped to see a stream off the volcano by now. Better yet, a tavern!"

Lasker said, "There will be water. I worry more about food. We were idiots not to pack a lunch before descending into the tunnel. And for not bringing some canteens of water!"

"Who forgot to pack *what,"* the Hermit smiled. And with those words he produced a small bundle of what looked like kiwi fruit out of his too-large robe. "I brought these fruits, which I raise in my cave. They grow well in the artificial light. These will restore our vitality for a time. They are both food and liquid. They're very juicy."

They all were pleased to accept two apiece, and they patted the old Hermit on the back as he distributed them. Lasker gave one of his to Dorjee, but she refused, saying, "Two is more than enough. I am smaller."

Lasker bit into one of them. The fruit was rather chewy and tasted like a blueberry. But it was juicy indeed. After a few chomps, he asked, "Say, just how do you raise *fruit trees* in that cave? I never saw such a thing, Hermit."

"They're not actually fruit, exactly. They're sort of mushrooms, really. Round, juicy, fruity mushrooms. But don't worry. They're fine to eat."

They chewed the sticky fruit-mushrooms with less enthusiasm after that statement. "Hey," Lasker said, trying to make the best of it. "Mushrooms or not, these would be a big hit in the States."

"But not in Tibet," Rinchen snorted. "We insist fruit comes from trees."

"Beggars can't be choosers," the Hermit snapped. "Eat and be happy you have them!"

After they were finished — there was no pit, of course, so they were quite sated and full — they quickly gathered some huge leaves from the bush and some twigs. They set up little sun-shield tents. Lasker's was a bit larger than the others, since he and Dorjee shared it.

Soon they all drifted off to sleep, Lasker cradling Dorjee in his arms in his makeshift shelter just a bit away from the others.

And none saw the pair of intense brown eyes peering at them from among the tangles of vines nearby. Nor the warpaint beneath those fierce and cunning eyes!

Chapter Thirteen

Safely out of sight of the others, and at last in relative darkness, away from the orange sun, Lasker pulled Dorjee to him. It was ecstasy feeling the sweet firmness of her so close. He thrilled at the pressure of this feminine body. It was familiar, yet unfamiliar. Dorjee was decidedly thinner. And of course there was the missing finger. Her hand had healed well, thanks to Cheojey and the Hermit's medicines.

She seemed remote. He asked, "Are you too tired?"

Dorjee said nothing for a time, kept her almond eyes averted, but she finally whispered, "I am not the same. I have been mutilated. Can you love me with my hand . . ." Tears welled up in her eyes.

"Dorjee," Lasker said, "look at me! You are the same, the woman I love. That missing finger is a badge of your courage. I love you even more."

She moaned sleepily in his arms and nibbled at his neck. Lasker felt the immensely thrilling fact of the throbbing life in her. The steady heavy beating in his chest was the drums of desire. The rising and falling of her breasts, her slow breathing, increased as they caressed.

He longed to make love to Dorjee right here and now, to strip off her clothing and make mad love. But she was far closer to sleeping than to sexual arousal. He mustn't press her now. She needed rest badly so he just held her softly, watched the slow rise and fall of her breast under the thin material of her inner garment. It was as if he held a child; a small and frightened child who was seeking comfort in the closeness. And he responded to that need.

Lasker had thought about a moment like this, a reunion with Dorjee, for a long long time. Many a night in Dharmsala he had stood at his window and watched the peaks of Tibet to the north and wondered if he would ever hold Dorjee again. And when he had found her alive in the lofty prison cell, he had exulted in that triumph. But things had happened since then: their flight of desperation away from a devilish and implacable enemy, danger and tensions that would have driven a lesser woman mad.

Never did he believe he would be holding Dorjee close to him in a tent of strange, large leaves, on the grass of a land he didn't know the name of, let alone the location! Pleasant dreams are made of gossamer dream-stuff, but this place of endless orange sunlight was more a nightmare than spun reveries.

She needed sleep. He contented himself with lightly stroking her hair, breathing her presence in. There would be time for lovemaking. When they were rested, when they were safe. She was back to him, alive, in his arms. That was all that mattered.

Lasker's mind drifted away to thoughts about fate and karma. What wild destiny had brought him and his lover here to this unknown land? Was there a purpose to this journey that was yet hidden? Would they survive this journey to return to the world they knew? Lasker had the same feeling, the same relentless premonition now that had been with him ever since they crawled out of the tunnel. A feeling that there was some sort of secret, an awesome, dangerous secret that he must unlock here in this bizarre land. The feeling that here — wherever *here* was — some strange danger must be faced, and overcome. And only then would the gods of destiny ever let him return to a land of sweet-smelling air and real day and night.

Lasker was dozing off, exhausted as he was. He thought he heard the changing of the guard outside. It seemed rather soon for the Hermit to be replaced by Rinchen, but time was so hard to determine when the sun never moved . . .

With that last thought he finally fell into deep dreamless sleep.

The Hermit, tired from long miles of walking, had dozed off, much to his peril. The stealthy movement through the grass was *not* Rinchen relieving him.

Yet Rinchen slept lightly, perhaps not trusting the old recluse to be on alert. In any case, he sat up abruptly in his makeshift tent and knew something was wrong. Rinchen *smelled* something alien from human flesh, with his highly attuned nostrils. Someone not in their party was nearby! He shimmied to the hole in the leaves and scanned the grassy clearing. Yes! His hawk-dark eyes detected a movement of the tall grass near the jungle-line. The figure was moving away. What had the briefly glimpsed, gray-haired figure been up to. How close had he been?

One thing for sure, Rinchen thought, the onlooker was not Bonpo. And human enemies were his meat and gravy!

The Tibetan strongman combat-crawled out to the dozing Hermit. Seeing he was fine, and snoring, Rinchen let him sleep. Then he crouch-ran to Lasker's tent. Rinchen paused but briefly to appreciate the tender scene of the two embraced. He hated to awaken them, yet he reached inside the leaf-tent and vigorously shook his American friend's shoulder.

Lasker's eyes popped open and focused on Rinchen, who explained in a whisper, "Bart, I think we're being watched."

Lasker slipped out of Dorjee's embrace and, as silently as possible, slid from the small tent. They moved some feet away and sat in a crouch. Rinchen pointed toward the trees.

"I don't see anything," Lasker pronounced after a while.

"Now! Over there!" Rinchen pointed somewhat to the left of the original sighting. Lasker saw a leaf waving slightly. That was all. "Just one man. The same one, I think," Rinchen whispered.

"What does he look like?"

"An old Indian. With war paint. Can we be in Arizona, Bart?"

"No. You know Arizona is desert, not jungle. But there are Indians elsewhere. In South America." Rinchen's eyebrow went up. "Don't worry about *that* now!"

They continued to scan the tree-line. And Lasker

spotted something. He almost didn't see him at first, as the figure stood so silently in the shadows of the palms. Then the tan, tall Indian raised an arm and waved. He plainly wished to be seen. Lasker saw that he was gray-haired, and had some brown streaks on his sunken cheeks. The streaks were more in the nature of decoration, Lasker thought, than war paint. He was stripped to the waist, and wore a short grass skirt. The Indian was carrying something in his other hand. A tube of some sort, a wooden straight tube.

Lasker had seen one of those tubes before. "He has a blowgun, Rinchen. But he means no harm. He could have used it on us already. See? There are fresh prints in the grass here. He was close, yet did nothing, took nothing. Wake the others, Rinchen," Lasker said. "I'll keep an eye on him."

As Rinchen crawled about awakening the others, Lasker studied the Indian who just stood still and occasionally waved. The man was quite old, maybe seventy or seventy-five. He had on some odd accoutrements: a necklace of amberlike stones, and a gourd hanging from his drawstring belt. Perhaps the gourd held water.

Water. How thirsty Lasker was! The elongated brown gourd was next to a string of dangling feathers of green and red and blue. The man's noble features and his outfit led Lasker to conjecture that he was staring at a South American Indian.

The gray-haired man bent down for a second. He put down the blowgun, and picked up something. He put it on his head. It sparkled with the glimmer of gold. It was an elaborate Inca-like headdress. And on its angular winged design was a many-legged snake, the same motif that Lasker had briefly seen at the tunnel exit.

Tsering touched Lasker's shoulder. "He put down the weapon," Lasker said. "That is a good sign."

"Everyone is alerted and ready to move on your signal. What do we do, Bart?" Tsering asked, wiping a furry red spider off his shoulder.

"I don't know. He seems anxious that we come over to him — look at the way he's gesturing."

Rinchen was down on his haunches on Lasker's other side now. He had his hand on his sword's hilt, and whispered, "I can circle around and kill him — if you keep his attention."

"No. Wait. Don't do anything unless he shows hostility. Maybe he is just a local who is curious about who we are, why we're here. We should be friendly. Offer him something."

Lasker hadn't finished the second of his mushroom-fruits. He stood up slowly and walked halfway toward the Indian, who didn't move. He put the fruit down, then walked back to his companions.

The Indian walked out and picked up the fruit and then untied the gourd from his belt and left that in the fruit's place. Then he went back to the trees.

Lasker quickly walked to the gourd, and lifted it. He pulled the plug and put the gourd to his lips. "Water!" he exclaimed, taking greedy slugs of the liquid.

The gourd was quite large, and each member of Lasker's party had a good swallow before it was empty.

"That fellow is okay by me," Rinchen muttered. "Let's go see what he wants. He's still waving to us to join him."

They smiled and walked warily toward the water-giver. The Indian turned and retreated a few steps, and

134

then turned back and waved again. "I think," said the Hermit, yawning widely, "that he wants us to follow him. And I say we should."

Lasker nodded. They slowly walked after the Indian who now began to lead them down a well-worn jungle path. The path led diagonally to the left, away from the looming volcano. Their guide seemed in no hurry. Indeed, it was as if he was trying *not* to lose them. Or maybe, Lasker thought, the guy was just too old to move fast.

"Where do you suppose he's taking us?" Dorjee asked.

Rinchen grumbled. "I hope it's a tavern! We have to eat sometime! What other choice do we have?"

"Rinchen is wise," the Hermit said. "I haven't seen any water. We have no food and we don't know what's poisonous and what isn't. If we don't find someone to help us survive — we'll die."

"Probably he's taking us back to his village," Lasker ventured. "I suppose that's all right. At least we'll find out where we are. I doubt there is any real danger, and we know he could have taken that blow tube he's carrying and darted us all while we slept. If he's no threat, we can reasonably hope his tribe isn't, either."

They followed their gray-haired guide for miles — maybe ten miles. The volcano loomed larger and larger, off to the side. Lasker could now see a bit of smoke issuing from the funnel at the top. The ground they walked on was rising. The village was on the slope of the volcano itself, Lasker realized.

They at last came upon water. A stream of intensely

cold water cascading down from the volcanic peak. The Indian ahead of them bent and cupped his hands and drank and then splashed his face. Then he turned, smiled at them, and pointed to the water. He moved off some paces.

They went to the stream and all drank heartily. And Dorjee filled the gourd. Lasker had to suppress a desire to jump into the icy water and immerse himself. There wasn't time for this!

The Indian was quickly off again, and they followed their silent guide up under a huge waterfall. The water cascading down with a tremendous roar had an odd rusty color. Lasker's party easily crossed the stream on the rocks that had been arranged conveniently to do just that, farther up the slope. It was still bright out, but Lasker's chronometer said three A.M.!

Eventually, after finding a path on the fall's other side — a path marked with skulls of some sort of lizard (or so Lasker thought), they came suddenly out onto a clearing. There were a dozen thatch-roofed huts in its center.

The village. No signs, no indication of location.

The old Indian shouted out something in a mystifying language of clicks and pops. He rushed across the grass at great velocity and he ran into the narrow entrance of a hut.

Lasker's party stood for a while at the treeline, and nothing else happened. No Indians appeared, nothing stirred. Lasker said, "We keep our guard up, but I think we should follow."

Lasker was first to step inside the open doorway. It was very dim inside the large hut, and empty. They had entered a huge mud-walled dome. The place was bare except for two statues in it. They were man-size, but didn't depict any human Lasker had run into. They were nude male figures, squarish-featured men made of soft stone. Each statue had huge erect penises sticking out at least two feet. They wore elaborate stone headdresses.

The workmanship was like the ancient Incas, Lasker decided.

A quick look around the hut showed no other exits save the one they came in by. Yet there was no evidence of the old Indian that had brought them there!

Lasker went over and studied one of the statues. On closer inspection, it was quite horrific. Its right hand was extended and holding a lifelike representation of a human head. The hair on that head seemed very lifelike. Lasker gingerly touched the face. Flesh! It was a real human head, one recently severed, and still soft-skinned.

As he shouted out his warning, there issued from a dozen points around the hut the rustle of sharp movements. And Lasker soon beheld that they were encircled by a hundred spear-and-blowgun-holding war-painted savages.

Chapter Fourteen

As more and more of the savages issued from the statue's base, they backed off.

"Where'd they come from?" Rinchen asked, mystified.

"Must be hidden passages here!" Lasker sized up their opponents. Many of the Indians wore what appeared to be remnants or reproductions of shiny conquistador armor. Surely this confirmed that Lasker's party had come up in some godforsaken corner of Peru or Bolivia. Many of the Indians had their short blowguns raised to their lips, and others had huge cleaverlike swords or bows with strings taut holding razor-tipped arrows trained on them. Lasker knew that it was time for negotiation, not confrontation. So he smiled, and said the one word that he hoped would ease the situation. Lasker said, *"Nosotros somos amigos."* He was addressing the one with the most feathers on his metal helmet. That helmet looked a lot like a conquistador's helmet. *"No problema,"* he added, then whispered, "Smile, everyone. My Spanish is piss-poor!"

They smiled like Chesire cats, and yet the Indians'

sour faces — make that *angry* faces — didn't change expression.

"Smiling ain't gonna be enough," Tsering said.

"Then we have to use these little explosive globes," the Hermit said, reaching slowly into his robe and extracting a few of the apple-size Cultivator explosives. "I have an idea. When I hand these to you, pretend to be chewing them. They look like fruit. Maybe they'll think we're eating a last meal before they wipe us out." The Indians looked uncertain.

Lasker watched the Hermit pretending to take a small bite of one of the "fruit." One of the Indians smiled and chuckled out something. Several of the others snickered. The Hermit was allowed to pass each of his party one of the explosive globes. He returned to place. "On my signal — throw them."

"In front of their feet, of course, you mean," Cheojey interjected, frightened that they would actually hurt someone.

The Hermit frowned. "Of course, Lama Cheojey. Of course."

Rinchen snorted and looked at Lasker, who said, "He's right! Don't hurt them."

"Now!" the Hermit yelled.

They all threw the Cultivator bombs, aimed at a spot halfway between the threatening Indians and themselves.

It was the oddest set of explosions Lasker had ever seen. The globes didn't make a sound when they exploded, yet Lasker and the others were thrown hard against the adobe wall behind them by the concussion. And the Indians likewise were tumbled down like winter wheat in a hurricane. The bombs blew a series of interlocking craters four feet deep and eight feet wide in the dirt floor — without leaving any debris or smoke. The ground simply vanished.

When the Indians scrambled to their feet, they were in an uproar. They started to reach for their weapons, but Lasker produced his last bomb from his pocket. Tsering, too, had one. That made them dive again to the floor, shouting in fright.

The invaders now seemed to have some respect. Their war-painted opponents were terrified and kept flat on the ground — for a long time. The bombs were not thrown. Eventually the one with all the red feathers and the conquistador helmet got up on his haunches. He uttered something that sounded plaintive and beseeching. Lasker motioned for the man to stand with a tight gesture. And he did. The other Indians, on some command uttered by the chief or whatever he was, all got on their knees and started bowing and wailing. They didn't stop for a long time.

"Well, at least we broke the ice with these guys," Lasker said wryly. "I don't think we'll have any more trouble with them."

Now the chief spoke: clicks and pops, then harsh syllables. Lasker understood that the chief was attempting to communicate in several different languages.

"What's he saying?" asked Tsering.

"I don't know," Lasker replied, shrugging his shoulders. "It's all Greek to me."

Now the chief raised an arm and pointed at the statue that held the human head. There was a peculiar sound — like a small horn blowing, and then the base of the statue slid open. A figure emerged. He was a man so tall that he had to bend to get through the seven-foot-high portal. The crowd parted as the tall one stepped forward, letting him approach Lasker and his friends.

This man was a different type entirely. He was very, very thin for one thing. And when the newcomer came to stand by the chief, he raised his staff—like a pharaoh's stick. When he smiled Lasker saw that he had green teeth. No not green. There were jade insets in his front teeth. This extremely tall man, obviously the head honcho around here, had a very peculiarly shaped head, most noticeable when he was in profile. The man's cranium extended back twice as far as a normal person's—hanging out over his shoulders. This was not his only peculiarity. He seemed to have practically no forehead.

The "chief" bowed and kissed the man's huge bare feet. Then he joined his fellow Indians who all were bowing to the newcomer. When all the Indians were prostrate, the tall man, picking his way carefully through the Indians, approached Lasker. Suddenly the very tall guy started speaking. Lasker broke out into a smile. So did Rinchen, Tsering, Cheojey. For the newcomer was speaking a fairly passable, though halting, *Tibetan!* "We are the Pukas," he said.

Lasker was able to reply, "I am Lasker. We come in peace. Understand?"

The man made a gesture with his two fingers raised—the universal sign of peace. He smiled his green jade best.

Lasker gave a wry wink to Tsering and the others. "I can handle this dude," he said, then began a rather slow but friendly dialogue. The tall man apologized for his speech. "I'm sorry my Tibetan is rusty. We've had little cause to use it for the past thousand years. I am supreme priest Jade Jaguar," he went on. "If my sub-chief Reemu has offended you great gods of the Upper Realm, let me remove him from thy sight!" He called the sub-chief over, and the man got on his knees mumbling something like apologies. The supreme priest started closing his long fingers about the man's throat. Lasker realized he was going to strangle the poor man.

Lasker said quickly, "We gods were not offended."

"What's going on?" Cheojey asked, missing some mispronounced words.

"I think he things we are great gods of some sort," the Hermit whispered. "This is very interesting."

Rinchen smiled. "This is more like it! So we're gods, huh?" The big man liked to hear that they were considered gods. That would offer certain advantages. You could almost see Rinchen's mind work! "Say, are there any women around here for us *gods?*" Rinchen asked. "And how about some Arak or at least chang, some whiskey or beer?"

Lasker said, "Hold your horses, Rinchen." His eyes rolled up. God! He hoped that Rinchen wouldn't blow it all by not acting godlike enough! "Let *me* talk!"

The tall man let go of the sub-chief, who bowed and scraped and kneed himself away, back into the crowd of kneeling Indians.

Well, this is nice, Lasker thought. It seemed that Lasker and Co. were now — as a result of the little bomb trick — taken for gods. The priest supreme rattled on about how wondrous it was that the gods had chosen to at long last answer the Puka prayers and emerge from the sacred well of the serpent.

143

Lasker played to that, saying, "Yes. We heard your call and took pity upon you."

Tsering whispered in Bart's ear, "Could you get us some food and water?"

Lasker didn't have to ask. The supreme priest soon offered to fete them, in the village center.

"Though we gods don't need it, of course, the gesture is appreciated and is accepted," Lasker replied, winking to Dorjee.

The supreme priest bowed his head and pointed toward the entrance. The Indians got out of the way, and the "gods" were led out of the building and onto a jungle path. There they saw their first Indian maidens, naked from the waist up. And very beautiful. The maidens threw flowers in their footsteps. Rinchen beamed. Finally they came to a clearing where a hastily arranged barbecue was being prepared. A giant boar was being set up on a pit over coals that were quickly fanned to a roaring flame by the bellows of the cooks. They had mats garlanded with flowers to sit upon, and someone started to play a stringed instrument.

At last they were poured drinks in jade goblets. Lasker tasted his. "I'd say this is passionfruit."

Cheojey sniffed it, ran a few drops around in his hands, and declared, "I think it's safe. The gods don't drink poison around here to prove their worth—I hope."

The priest sat next to Lasker, who because of his size or possibly because he was the only one who spoke directly to the priest, was considered the head god. Lasker was soon able to ascertain from speaking to Jade Jaguar that the Puka were the remnants of the Incas. They had fled to Macchu Piccu, their last

Andean stronghold, and then the gods took them to this place called Shaumb. The Incas forsook their old language, but not their religion. In the hundreds of years since that escape, no one had ever found them, and the gods had not returned — until now.

"How many entrances to this land are there?" Lasker asked. Maybe there was another way back — an easier way than going through what must be a Bonpo-infested tunnel by now!

The priest, looking suspicious, said, "Three, of course. One from Khufu-pyramid, one from Macchu Piccu, and the third from the sacred well that lies up in the snow mountains of holy men."

"Careful," Cheojey admonished, whispering, "We gods should know these things.

Lasker nodded. He had made a mistake. He'd better not make too many. That reference to the snow mountain would be Tibet — the tunnel they came through, Lasker realized. "Just a test of your knowledge, Jade Jaguar," Lasker said. "You are correct."

Jade Jaguar took a deep breath. He seemed happy to have met the gods' test and passed. He stood up and rattled off in some other language to his followers to bring forth plates of the boar, now roasted to a fare-thee-well.

Bart tried to be composed, but he gobbled down the food like he was a mortal who was mighty mighty hungry. They all did.

The priest asked about Dorjee. "Surely the gods are male. What is the woman doing among you?"

Lasker said, "She is a male in the illusory appearance of a woman." He hoped that would do, but it sounded lame.

145

The priest looked at Dorjee very carefully. He seemed confused momentarily and then began to laugh. "The gods make a joke with me."

After that Lasker laughed and so did the rest of his party. Word spread and all the Pukas were laughing.

That was a very close call, Lasker thought. After that he shut up before he could make another mistake and get them parboiled. Their lives depended on continuing to be considered gods, he was sure of that.

"Pretty swell party," said Rinchen, downing another of the potent root-brews — some sort of beer, according to the Hermit, who did a fair job on the brew himself. Rinchen was eyeing the maidens.

"Don't drink too much of that stuff," Cheojey admonished. "None of you! I don't know if the gods get affected by alcohol."

"I'll watch it," Lasker said, putting down his glass. "But after all that trekking and all that danger, I just couldn't resist whetting my whistle."

Cheojey kept serious-minded, saying, "Don't you think we had better get away from here? All that music and drumming and the smoke of the fire are bound to attract the Bonpo."

"So what?" Tsering said. "We can send a horde of these buddies of ours out against them. These guys will do anything we say!"

"Yeah," Lasker frowned, "but what happens if these Indians think the Bonpo are *other* gods!"

Chapter Fifteen

The feast went on hour after hour. The male Indian dancers covered with feathers came out in a line and impersonated various birds—strutting, pecking, running and leaping, singing—quite convincingly. The older women sat to the side and played the small flutes, which had a unique property. They had strings of animal gut on them, so they were stringed instruments as well. The results were many birdlike sounds.

Then to Rinchen's delight some of the Indian maidens—totally naked but painted red—came and did some wild gyrations. Then as most of them ran giggling away, he tripped up a pair of them, who seemed to be twins. As they laughed and giggled, Rinchen drew them to sit alongside him.

Lasker worried that this show of human desire would screw things up, but the Indians clapped and shouted, and Rinchen pawed away.

The supreme priest sitting next to Lasker said, "Your god-friend does us honor to have two of our daughters sit with him. We hope he will do the greater honor of *seeding* them, come the end of the feast."

Lasker smiled. "I don't think Rinchen-god will disappoint your tribe."

"That is good. Did you like the men's bird dance? Was it done properly?"

"Oh, yes. Magnificent," Lasker said.

"Ah, I am so pleased. We, as you know," he said, "worship birds because they are capable of soaring off the ground. Like you gods," he added.

"Yes . . . of course," Lasker said, hoping that he wouldn't have to fly for these natives. Since everything seemed under control, he watched as the dances continued. This time the men formed a circle doing small birdlike hops. As he sipped the liquor and bit the pieces of succulent boar, his mind drifted away from the immediate situation to their general problems. The Bonpo were after them, for one thing. For another thing—where were they? Most of all, why didn't it ever get dark? It was very disconcerting that the "sun" behind the roiling clouds hadn't moved an iota. That the orange light beyond those roiling pink clouds didn't get any weaker. Where the hell was Shaumb?

Dorjee was asleep, leaning against him. The food and the wine had sated her, and she was drowsy.

Lasker decided to chance asking a few more questions. "Jade Jaguar, why doesn't the sun move?"

The supreme priest looked worried for a second and then replied, "Because it doesn't. Is that the right answer, oh god from the well?"

"Yes, of course. But did the sun ever move? Do you know what night is—darkness, a time without sun?"

The supreme priest looked awed. "Only the gods know of such a place! Is it like that where the gods live? Does the sun move there?"

"Yes," Lasker said, much puzzled. Evidently this guy thought it peculiar that there could be darkness. What the hell was going on in this screwy country? Where the hell were they anyway? And most important, how could they leave here?

Lasker leaned back on the flower-strewn cushions and scanned the sky. He saw a few birds that looked like seagulls but moved very slowly. Then he saw a strange green flickering. It had just now begun, low in the sky, in the opposite direction of the volcano. That sickly green was familiar to him—too familiar.

"What is that green flickering in the sky?" Lasker asked the high priest.

"The energy that feeds the god-world above," the priest intoned. "So you are testing me again? I hope I have answered correctly."

"Yes, I am testing you," Lasker said, then leaned over away from Dorjee and asked Cheojey in a low voice, "What do you think Jade Jaguar means?"

Cheojey put down his stalk of "celery" and whispered, "I know one thing—that green energy is some evil force of immense proportions. Its color is much like the Bonpo energy-fields. I don't think the high priest will give anything but enigmatic answers. Perhaps if the sub-chief Reemu is asked, he will expand on what the priest told you. By the way," Cheojey said, raising his voice, "try the vegetables. They're very good."

"So's the roast pork," Lasker added heartily. Again lowering his voice to a whisper, "But you're right. The sub-chief seems to have his feet on the ground more than this guy. I'll ask him," Lasker said. "Maybe I can at least find out what *continent* we're on!" Gently Lasker rearranged Dorjee on the cushions. Her long silken black

149

hair fell forward slightly. He had a rush of tenderness for her. She looked so small and helpless lying there.

He slowly stood up and stretched. He could hear hearty laughter. Rinchen was having a hell of a time! As he passed, he observed Rinchen with his arms full of the appreciative maiden twins. Tsering was pie-eyed drunk and nodding. Almost out cold, it seemed. The Hermit was studying some loose-page books that a scholarly man was handing him, to the side of the party.

Lasker motioned and drew the sub-chief over. He handed Reemu a horn full of the root-alcohol drinks, and that flattered the man a bit. Lasker prevailed upon the already drunken sub-chief to brag about his tribe's accomplishments. "I'll bet," Lasker said, "that you have been close to the source of the green fire in the sky." His words were understood well enough, this time.

The Indian sub-chief smiled. "Ah yes, we have traveled far—to the land of the giant beasts and beyond." He explained to Lasker that "the green fire," as he called it, was hundreds of miles away. "My clan has traveled to the end of the river to the north," he said, "but no farther. The green in the sky was intense there. Baalzabub came and stood on the banks and warned us away."

"Who is he?"

"We go to him for advice," the sub-chief explained, "but he always meets us on the riverbank and warns us to go no farther. Baalzabub says the green comes from a great silver object not of this world. He says it was the source of power in the otherworld, the world that the gods, yourselves, come from. You are," he smiled, "testing me, I know! Great One, tell me: have you gods come to go visit that power? Baalzabub said we should pray for the gods to come and destroy it. I don't understand that, but then I am a mere mortal."

Lasker asked the chief about anything else he could say about the green power, forgetting about questions of location.

The answer was disappointing this time. "No one knows what causes the rays. All we know is that it comes from far upriver in the deepest unexplored jungle — past the sacred home. Baalzabub is the last practitioner of the old religion. Only those mortals that partake of the rebirth ordeal can know such things. And then only in their dreams that quickly fade away. Is this not why you have brought the female being with you, oh god of light and fire? Is she not the mortal who will dream of the location of the green fire? So she may tell our tribe its mysteries in ways we mortals understand? Will not this female named Dorjee partake of our rebirth ceremony, and tell of the green mystery?"

Lasker was taken aback. But he mumbled out, "You answer well," and left the man. Lasker was more perplexed than ever. He moved back along the edge of the celebrations and over to the lama, as the dancers and singers went on entertaining — and Rinchen was encouraging Jade Jaguar to share some native brew — distracting the high priest. He explained to Cheojay what he surmised from the sub-chief's words: "We've stumbled upon the source of the Bonpo power! Some silver object in this place!"

When the male line dancers were again dancing madly, Lasker gathered and conferred with his friends. "We have to find out more about this Baalzabub and the green power."

The Hermit said, "Maybe we'll have to take the chance

151

of having Dorjee go through this rebirthing."

"No! I won't have it," Lasker replied.

The Hermit touched his sleeve. "Let her. We have to know where we are and what's going on here. I believe the key thing we need to know is why the sun doesn't move! We have to know, Bart. Let her do it. There are too many things unknown here!"

Lasker looked over to Dorjee, who was now sitting languorously against a palm and dozing, so *beautifully*. How could he ask her to partake in a savage ritual, perhaps risk her life, after all she had been through?

"I'll ask her," he sighed.

Chapter Sixteen

Lasker gently shook Dorjee awake and told about the rebirth ceremony. She was eager to take part in the practice. "Let me do it, Bart. I want to! I am strong; I can handle it." She sat up alert, enthusiastic. "I *will* do the ceremony. Don't you see, this is my chance to be of some use!"

"It could be dangerous."

She was adamant, would not change her mind, and Lasker reluctantly had to agree. He went to inform Jade Jaguar that Dorjee would partake of the rebirthing dream. Under the supervision of himself—a god, who wished to check that the ceremony would be done "properly." "Now, please explain it, Jade Jaguar."

The priest said, "I will explain. Since time immemorial, the Puka have known that every being has a physical self and a dream self. The dream self is not limited. It can travel without boundary, and know what the gods know. It is more real and everlasting than our bodies."

Lasker smiled. "Correct. Go on."

Jade Jaguar recited, "The Creating-Woman who gave birth to the gods and to the earth, which, was seeded by the serpent who sang into being the human creatures that are here. She also sang into being our tribe, and then the red salamander. She made the salamander so we might know of her and of the meaning of our lives. Each generation one of our people dreams the dream of life and understands and retells us the truth of allness. Otherwise, we might forget, and think that we are real. Only the dream is real."

"Correct," Lasker said. He still hadn't found out if this dreaming was dangerous. "And what happens to the dreamers?"

"They awaken, tell their tale, and go back into the dream forever. Their bodies rot like all matter, their spirits soar. We decapitate them."

Lasker felt a knot clench his stomach. "Do any dreamers live?"

"Not unless they are wrapped in the leaf of the Reviving-Tree. They prefer to go back into the dream, to die. So, very few are put in the leaves. Only those who are not worthy are denied death."

"Jade Jaguar, I want those leaves for Dorjee. She is not to die after the dream. Understand?"

"This is most unusual, but you are to be obeyed. Is it a punishment to her? Did she offend you so much that you will not let her dream forever?"

Lasker didn't answer, which impressed the hell out of the high priest.

Jade Jaguar bowed. "We shall go harvest the reviving leaves. I will return in the time of seven thousand heartbeats." Lasker did a quick calculation. Seventy heartbeats a minute. Let's see, seven thousand heartbeats is one hundred minutes. "Okay. Do that."

Meanwhile the whole village was excited. The sub-chief, Reemu, called forth the tribal maidens, all virgins, to prepare Dorjee. "The hair-braiding, cleansing, and skin-coloring will be done by the time the leaves are here," Reemu promised.

"Very well, but I'll watch," Lasker said, "to make sure all is done correctly, of course."

"Come," the sub-chief said. He shook his rattle and led Dorjee to the great statue of the salamander. "This is the place of the awakening of dreams. Bathe in this sacred fount of water first. Then we will begin." The sub-chief left her to the maidens and Lasker-god. Dorjee stripped and bathed in the red "pool of blood," as they called it. Actually, Lasker, realized it was iron ore in the water. Then the youngest girl carried forth one red lizard. It looked like the statue. It was a tiny, harmless-enough-looking salamander. Lasker had observed that the unmoving lizards were all over the statue. They probably ate insects. They put the little lizard in a bejeweled box.

There were drums as Jade Jaguar returned from the forest with the leaves, which resembled giant tobacco leaves. They smelled funny. "Put them over there — in the dreaming hut." Jade Jaguar said, "She is cleansed. Now all you must leave except the chief god — Lasker." His friends went behind the rock.

As Lasker watched for any signs of danger to Dorjee, the maidens braided her hair, gently cooing encouraging words into her ears. Dorjee was given a grass skirt, but remained naked to the waist. The woman with the lizard-box opened it, put the red lizard against Dorjee's chest — between her breasts. It clung there. Dorjee watched the lizard calmly as they all backed off.

There was a flash of smoke from the lizard and then

she screamed and collapsed. Lasker was instantly at her side and tore the salamander away. He could see that it had burned her.

Jade Jaguar intoned, "It is done. It is good," as Dorjee's eyes rolled up and she slumped over.

"What is done? Is she dead?" Lasker was not feeling like a god now. He felt for her pulse. He couldn't detect a single heartbeat. He put his ear to her chest. "God, what have you done to her?"

"She will dream now. She is not dead. As testimony of her bravery, she will have that lizard-curve, like a small half moon, forever—a tattoo. The chemical goes through her system and she thus swoons." The high priest clapped his hands twice and Dorjee was lifted in a litter and carried to the dreaming hut, where she was placed on a mat on the floor. When the litter-bearers had left, the high priest and Lasker entered the hut.

Dorjee now looked and acted as if she had a fever. Her face was alternately flushed and then pale. Her eyes would flutter open, unseeing pupils dilated. She moaned. She perspired heavily, her braided hair became matted. "This dream had better be good!" snapped Lasker, who was truly frightened by her appearance. The drums went on and on, growing ever more insistent. The supreme priest kept walking about the mat, chanting and shaking rattles, as if to frighten the evil demons away. Suddenly Dorjee's body became rigid. Lasker's heart leapt into his throat. "Is she dead?"

"No. She dreams. Now you will wrap her in the reviving leaves and she will dream, and then will come alive again. Isn't that right, oh god, Lasker?"

Lasker controlled himself. "That is right." But to himself he thought, *Oh, God, it better be.*

Dorjee felt herself being carried, but didn't care where. The hut became like a picture, a flat picture. And then flipped around and spun and shrunk. She was someplace else. Another world.

She heard the drumbeats, no—they were her heartbeats, no—the heartbeat of *all* living things! Now, Dorjee saw dream-images; a giant tree reaching into clouds. She was standing at the bottom of it. It was beautiful. It was the Eden-place—Shambhala. She tried to climb up, but the trunk was too big around to grasp. Suddenly she saw a spider climbing up into it. It became very large or she became small. But she got on its back. Up, up the spider climbed, its sticky little feet never missing a step.

"Where are you now, Dorjee? What do you see?" Lasker asked, tugging on her hand hoping to get her attention, to see signs of awareness.

"No. Don't pull me back. I'm climbing up a tall tree on the back of a spider," Dorjee muttered, swishing her head about violently.

"What do you see on or in the tree?"

"The tree has good fruit and bad—right and left; and lots of pretty-colored birds and monkeys. It is the tree of life."

"What's at the top of the tree?"

"The devil. The man that the Christians, the stiff-collars, call the devil."

"The devil?"

"He will know the answers. He will *know*," Dorjee

157

insisted, lost in her reverie. "He will know why the sun doesn't move. It is very important to see him. We are here at his call. The devil called us!"

"Why has he called us, Dorjee?" Lasker didn't like this at all!

"What a view the tree has! You can see so far away. It's so beautiful. There's a bird. I'm riding on its back. Now I am the bird. I am flying up the river, over mountains far away. Yes, now I see a shiny metallic object. It's so big! It must be miles long!" Dorjee started laughing, almost maniacally.

"What about the metal thing?"

"It is evil. I can feel it. I am afraid," she said, looking pained.

"Go closer, Dorjee. Is there anything else?"

"There is a green glowing — sort of skull. Only it isn't."

"Isn't what?"

"I see a great swirling skull made of energy not matter. This is the source of the evil power. Oh! The green-robed people! We must defeat the green-robed people. We must go to the man with the trident for directions. We must see him first, or we will die!"

"Where is he? Do you mean this man who is the devil?"

"At the top of the tall tree! Far far upriver, past the land-of-steam. The place we must cross to go to Baalza-bub." At the end of this statement, Dorjee's body again went limp, into a swoon imitating death.

"Dorjee are you all right?" Her body felt stone cold. Lasker went to the door of the hut where he found Cheojey waiting patiently. "See to her, Cheojey. If they've harmed her in any way, I'll — "

Rushing in without further ado, brushing past Jade

Jaguar, Cheojey took her pulse and opened her eyes. "She is barely alive," Cheojey said. "Quick, we must cleanse her, purge her." Cheojey made her vomit with his finger in her mouth, and then drink some of his fruit mix. Cheojey had tested certain native fruits and made an antidote! Finally her eyes began to flutter. She came around and smiled. "I dreamt. It was wonderful. I want to go back! Please!"

"No. Please. Stay here." Lasker wondered what part of her dream was reliable. And if it all was—he had a definite aversion to following the bidding of a devil!

After some steaming cups of bark-tea, Dorjee was able to sit up. Her pulse steadied, her fever declined. She said, "I flew there, Bart. I *flew!* It was wonderful! I saw it, the silver palace containing the *power*, in my dream. All we have to do is go to the big tree where the man with the trident lives. He'll tell us what we need to do to stop the evil."

"I know. You told me everything as you dreamt it."

"I *did* have the weird feeling that I wasn't quite alone."

Dorjee was still recovering when there was an uproar outside. "Watch her, Cheojey," Lasker said. He stepped outside to investigate the commotion. "What's up?"

Soon he returned to tell the others, "A runner has come. He was a lookout near where we picked up the Indian we followed. He says that a band of strange beings—possibly also gods—are bypassing the village—going toward the green fire."

"The Bonpo!" the Hermit exclaimed. "They did not come to this land after *us!* Though they will destroy us, if they can. They are going to the source of their new-found power."

"To fix it," Dorjee stuttered out. "The thing is uncertain . . . It is irregular. Something," she said, "something must be done to secure it. Yes, I saw the silver temple. A long, low dome. There is a . . ." She gasped. "A giant glowing skull there."

"That means we have got to get the hell there first," Lasker said. "We go to destroy this energy-skull. Dorjee, can you walk?"

"Yes, I feel fine as a matter of fact. I feel like all my tiredness has disappeared. I feel—born again!" She smiled.

Lasker went alone to speak to Jade Jaguar. In a short while he returned to the recovery hut and announced: "It's all set. I convinced them all to come along with us, telling them they will be killed by the others. I told them that the Bonpo are evil beings, not gods. I said we will allow the Puka to accompany us on our god-mission to destroy the evil skull. For their own safety."

"Neat," the Hermit said, using the colloquial English that so annoyed Lasker, "and essentially true."

"We head to the river. There are supposed to be a group of war canoes there, for heading upstream."

Chapter Seventeen

The party set out as soon as the porters, burly women seemingly bred for carrying burdens, were assembled. They would carry tenting and food for an extended trip. Eight of the best Puka warriors, led by their high priest, the sub-chief, plus Lasker and company, strode just ahead of them.

There was a wide jungle path for several miles and then they came to a green river of still waters. There were ten long canoes pulled up on a slate-flake beach. The canoes, Lasker noted, were big jobs. Each was about fifty feet long, and seamless. They were like long peapods. He found them preposterously narrow.

Cheojey, too, had been intrigued by the canoes. He bent to examine the material of which they were constructed and announced, "Made of some extremely strong bark, the bark of a single split tree"

The women bearers packed the gear aboard very carefully, making sure of the balance. They pulled the canoes free of the beach and waded out knee-deep. On a signal, all boarded at the same time, to keep the canoes on an even keel. Then everyone else got on board. The sitting would be in rows. No two abreast was possible. Eight of the canoes were full to the brimming, the other two lay on the beach.

Just as they had all boarded, a rear lookout came running and panted out, "The evil ones are less than five minutes away down the path."

"Let's move then," Lasker said. "Drag the two empty canoes along with us, then scuttle them."

The sub-chief started to protest in his bad Tibetan, but Lasker gave him a sharp look and he subsided.

Jade Jaguar said nothing. He had taken to the prow of the first canoe and sat erect and tall, looking upriver.

Once the canoes were a dozen yards from shore, Lasker was the first to jab a sword into the empty boat alongside his canoe. Rinchen finished off the other empty bark. And then they ordered swift rowing. The burly women were eager to comply.

The paddles were short and broad, so their pace was soon rapid. But Lasker was surprised that rather than go midriver, the warrior ruddermen kept the canoes close to shore. "Why don't we go in midchannel," Lasker asked the high priest, who sat just ahead of him.

"Big snake creatures," Jade Jaguar said, "giant anacondas out there, with bodies thick as trees. So it is best to keep within fifteen feet of the shore."

Lasker didn't complain. He had worried about the Bonpo running along the shore and shooting their arrows. But the jungle along the river was so thick no one could follow. And they were miles gone from the launch-beach by the time the enemy could have possibly reached it.

There was one worry: The Bonpo had strong magic. And that blasted energy-skull, whatever it was. Could they *create* boats? Or even if they couldn't, how quickly could the Bonpo fell trees and make more? He settled back, leaning on the low cushion for that purpose, and watched the lazy river float by. The green flickering in the sky was clearly visible. Like waves of energy. It was a strange combination—the green flickers, the orange cloudcover. Surely this was all a dream, and Lasker would soon wake up in the Dharmsala library, and rue the fact that he had too much arak the night before to study. Yes, that was it—*a dream*. Lasker half closed his eyes. It *had* to be a dream: the alien subway, the conductor with a thousand teeth, the Puka Indians, the ritual death of Dorjee . . . The whole bit was obviously a crazy dream.

But when a double-winged bird flitted overhead and dropped a wet turd on his face, causing the women rowers nearest him to giggle, the Great God Lasker knew he *wasn't* dreaming. After a shout, Lasker laughed, too, and Dorjee, immediately behind him, dipped a cloth in the water and rinsed his face.

He relaxed again. The hazy orange sun flickered off the moving waters, the breeze cooled and soothed him. It was very pleasant to be traveling this way; easy on the feet for a change.

Dorjee, seemingly fully recovered from her ordeal, more alive than ever, held him around his waist. They just glided along as if with not a care in the world, the gentle wind stirring his long dark-brown locks.

Jade Jaguar kept an eagle-eyed watch. He kept scanning the river ahead for any of those big snakes. Or so he said. Lasker wondered about the high priest. Was he more, or less, than he said he was? Sometimes his reactions seemed very human. Sometimes he was cold as ice. The only one that Jade Jaguar really seemed to like was his drinking buddy, Rinchen. He kept waving to him.

The river journey lasted three days — three days of sleeping on the sandy beaches, which sometimes were found at the river's sharp curves; three days of seemingly endless rowing on the quiescent river. Lasker's watch insisted there had been three days without nights! But the Indians had gourd equivalents of hourglasses. Lasker had picked one that was twelve hours in measure. He estimated that fact by measuring the movement of the grain against his pulse beat for more than twenty minutes, not relying on his chronometer at all. The hourglass could be off an hour or two, but what the hell . . . better than nothing. Better than a *crazy* wristwatch.

The Indians, Lasker believed, normally slept only every four or five days. They found the rest habits of the gods rather a nuisance, but they put up with it, often playing a silent game of something like pickup sticks, while Lasker's party snored away on the beach. Jade Jaguar never laid down.

On the riverbank, strips of wild pig meat were cooked over a small fire. As little smoke as possible. This was done wherever any dried driftwood could be had. Most of the vegetation was damp and juicy — too juicy to make a clean fire.

The best part of the journey was the fact that Lasker and company, being gods, didn't have to row.

Eventually, the river became muddy, shallow, and windingly narrow. It was becoming a swamp, in fact.

Dorjee, while she acted normal at all times, was

convinced that she was still in a trance and could direct them. Once the river became a dozen channels, she said which channel they must head down. They traveled a zigzag course for several more "hours" until their particular stream was just a trickle, and the rowers were reduced to using their paddles to pole the bottom, to make progress. Double-winged birds plunged for twin-tailed red carp.

"Are you sure we're not lost, Dorjee?" Lasker asked.

"No, we're not lost," she smiled. "This is the way, as I saw it in my dreamtime. This is as far as we can go for now. We get off here."

Lasker sighed. If her dream was wrong, or if she remembered it incorrectly, they were lost. They made the bank and tied the canoes to some twisted roots.

"Where do we go now?" Lasker asked, helping her ashore.

Dorjee said, "Nowhere. We just wait."

So they waited. And waited.

"Why don't we go someplace?" Rinchen asked, passing a bottle to Jade Jaguar.

"Because," Dorjee explained, "there is nothing but quicksand between here and Baalzabub's house. We must have water to sail further. The rain will come soon. In the meantime, we must wait. The old man Baalzabub will send rain."

They natives set up the large leaf tents and they all rested. A day passed, then two. Lasker was getting looks from the sub-chief, and he was antsy himself. Jade Jaguar didn't seem to mind waiting. He shared some more native liquor with Rinchen and listened to the strongman's wild tall tales. He didn't tell any stories of his own, and when asked why, the high priest said he had a bad memory for things past. "Very said," said Rinchen. "Have another drink.

The Hermit was in a tizzy. He stormed back and forth along the banks of the muddy water casting spells and cursing. Nothing happened. He had considerable powers back in Tibet to create wind and rain and storm, as a *ngapa*. But here he seemed powerless to help out.

And then on the third day — six twists of the gourd — it rained. And it rained and rained. Dorjee danced and laughed in the warm downpour. She splashed around like a little girl in the rising waters.

It was a peculiar, very hot rain, Lasker thought. Where the hell were they that the sun never set, and the rain was so hot? He wanted to see this so-called wise man Baalzabub very badly. He needed answers, even from a devil!

The rain soon swelled the river, and they packed up, drenched to the skin, and set forth once more via canoe. Lasker was worried about all that rain filling their peapod-crafts. But he found out that they didn't need to bail water. The Indians drew out wide animal skins to cover over any open areas amidst passengers and cargo. The rowers had to use all their considerable muscles now against the current, but they were up to it. At Dorjee's shouted directions, they headed this way or that way, up the winding channels.

"We're getting close," Dorjee announced, just as the rains let up. "Set the canoes on the beach over there." She pointed to a black gravel area along a bank. "The land is solid from here on," Dorjee said, "and it isn't a far walk."

"Then we walk," Lasker said, "very rapidly."

They did their best to hide the bark canoes in the foliage near the little beach, and then the safari snaked

166

onward by foot.

The jungle faded away, to be replaced by a dry sandy plain full of swirling dust-devils. "The steam-lands I saw are just ahead," Dorjee cautioned. "It will be hard for us."

Indeed, it soon looked less and less like Eden and more like hell. There were sounds in the earth like boiling, and thunder, and great geysers of brown steam—steam mixed with mud—roared heavenward just a hundred yards ahead of them.

Lasker called a brief halt to their movement and announced, "This is the bad part. We're at the Steamlands, Dorjee says. We have to keep together, follow her. There are blow-holes all over, some active, some not. Be careful of your footing. Now let's go."

As they walked on, between geysers of erupting mud and rock, through sulphurous gasses and foul mists, Lasker decided *this* was the most fiendish landsscape he'd ever seen. It was a treacherous area, full of all the traps of hell itself.

Tremors shook the land, great cracks moved open or closed, and the Indians were truly terrified. Only Dorjee's insistence that they would all survive if they stuck together—relayed though Lasker's words shouted over the titanic tumult—steadied them.

The key word "stick together" fell on deaf ears at the rear of their line. Two of the bearers, less brave than the others, had moved slowly, dropping back in fear. Now, before anyone could go back for them, there was a scream. Lasker whirled about and saw one of the woman disappear as a jet of steam caused the ground at her feet to give way. The second woman panicked at the sight and ran right into the bottomless bowels of a quiescent blowhole. They were not seen again.

Lasker shouted, "Move on. Keep together. You will live if you follow instructions. "His hair stood on end as he held onto Dorjee. She led them between a dozen eruptions of lava-dotted steam. For a moment, they were completely encircled by the awesome geysers of death. Hot steam and mud cascaded up and fell on them, searing their exposed skin. It looked to Lasker like it was all over! They'd never meet Baalzabub, nor find out where they were. Nor would they much care! They'd be dead as boiled lobsters in a second.

Chapter Eighteen

Into the valley of death by fire and asphyxiation they walked, arms linked. Sometimes a voice cried out, as when a red hot rock pummeled a head, or when scalding water sprayed on someone. But not one of the party got separated again. And somehow, someway, the most intense blasts of hellfire were left behind.

They moved on chastised, bruised, with raw burns on the exposed arms and legs of several members. Their faces were covered with the spatter of gray-brown mud, their hair choked with sticky, rapidly condensing and hardening clay. But they were out of the Steam-lands. Dorjee's dream had been correct—so far.

Lasker finally said, "We can spread out again, if we watch our step." He sized up their losses—the two women bearers, and most of the other bearers' burdens. Only a little food left, a few twigs for fire—and, thank the gods, a few gourds filled with sweet water. Lasker, stepping gingerly between small, inactive steam blow-holes, inhaled, and breathed fresh air once again. You never know how wonderful it is, until you don't have any!

Soon they came upon real earth, not the loathsome deposits of salt and magma. And shortly after that, they trod over stubby red grass. They were on a rolling plain again, and there appeared a huge misty shape on the horizon. A squarish hill—like a mesa, Lasker thought.

"There!" Dorjee cried out. "There is the Eden tree! There we will find Baalzabub."

Lasker strained his eyes but he still saw nothing except the huge hill-shape. "Where?" he asked.

She pointed. "Don't you see? It is so big, how can you miss it?"

Only then did he realize that the hill *was* the tree. It covered half his field of view, shimmering in gray mists. It was so damned big he hadn't taken it for a tree. They walked onward, and the mists grew thicker, condensed to rain—a downpour that cleansed them and seemed to soothe their singed skin areas as well. It took hours to reach their goal, by which time they were dry.

The tree was like a giant broccoli stalk reaching into the clouds above. "The trunk," Tsering exclaimed, "must be hundreds of feet wide! And those branches don't even begin until just below the clouds. How high is it?"

"High enough that we had better find the easy way up," Lasker said softly. Dorjee's expression was serene. For twenty minutes or so, they stood under the canopy of high branches. And that was a very humbling thing to do. The bark was smooth and hard, no way to climb it unless they dug in spikes and, even then, who could climb so far? And for what?

"The great one, the old man called Baalzabub," Dorjee said with reverence in her tones, "lives up there in a strange wooden house. I know you can't see it from

170

here, but it's there. In my dreamtime, I touched the boards of the house. It is there."

They all stood and craned their necks. Occasionally a strange shriveled fruit fell like a meteor from above. The Indian bearers bent and tasted, then ate them. "How do we get up there, Dorjee? Where is that spider that is supposed to take us up?" Not that Lasker really wanted to meet any spider of the size that could carry them.

The sub-chief pushed close to Lasker. "Won't you gods fly up? Why don't you just fly up?"

Lasker, feeling the sarcasm in the sub-chief's words, improvised an answer, "It is not our way to fly now. You do not understand that we wish to be as you are, mere humans, for a time."

The sub-chief frowned. He walked away mumbling discontentedly. Lasker decided he'd have to keep a close eye on the man from here on in. Probably their performance in the Steam-lands wasn't nearly godlike enough for sly Reemu. And after all, the Indians had all seen "the gods" eat and piss, and even sneeze. How could they not be suspicious that they might not be gods?

"Better pray for a ladder hidden somewhere," whispered Cheojey. "I think we'd better get up there before they skewer us."

Dorjee was acting strange again. She sang lullabies to herself and danced among the mushrooms and fallen branches. She didn't seem to quite be focused on the danger.

There was a creaking above — and as Lasker looked up a platform appeared, descending from the mists of the canopy above. "There," sang Dorjee, "is the spider that will take us up."

Lasker was very thankful that it wasn't a spider but

just a platform made of branches and roots woven together like a bird's nest. It did *look* a bit spiderlike, descending on its one strong central rope, though, as it had eight or ten poles arranged at its baselike legs. Perhaps they were to level it on the irregular ground below.

It dropped rapidly and made quite a thud when it hit the ground. It looked very much like a gazebo had plopped down from heaven.

"Only the gods — and Jade Jaguar, of course — will get in on this trip," the Hermit announced. He, too, evidently had become aware of the sullen unrest among the eight warriors, and some of the burly women bearers. The hermit had a good idea, Lasker thought. This was an ideal way to leave their troubles behind.

"I want to go too," the sub-chief called out. "There is room for one more."

Jade Jaguar raised his long arm and put his palm toward the sub-chief. "It is enough that I go up and represent the Puka tribe."

The sub-chief bowed, but not too low. Lasker's party, plus Jade Jaguar, climbed toward the aerial gazebo and, without them doing a thing, it started upward at a good clip.

On the way up they passed some lower branches. There sat several large red birds with double wings. And the drooping branches held what looked like shriveled prunes. Lasker grabbed one as the platform swayed near to one branch, and bit into the fruit. "Hmmm, these are good!"

Rinchen was pallid, and he kept looking at Jade Jaguar's undisturbed face for reassurance. They had been rising for a long, long time, and very fast indeed!

Lasker knew what Rinchen was thinking: *"If the rope broke now . . ."*

They suddenly reached their stop. Their elevator had deposited them level with a pathway secured among the thick branches — a plank walkway into the forest of the tree's heavy canopy.

"Top floor," the Hermit joked. "Lingerie, leaves, and holy men! Everyone off!"

Rinchen was first to clamber onto the boards. They bent under his weight. "Where to?" he asked. "This is worse than flying."

Lasker shrugged. Nobody was around, and the only sounds were the cries of the angry jay-birds. Or so he thought.

"I'm already here," a soft voice said from among the leaves behind them. Lasker spun around to see a young man. Much younger than anyone he'd expected. He was as robust and barrel-chested as his great tree, and well-muscled. He wore a faded red diaperlike loincloth and his chest was all covered with curly red hair, matching that on his head. He had on sandals, completing the effect that Lasker decided was closest to an Irish wrestler. He looked menacing because of the scowl he wore. And the spotted red snake draped around his neck didn't help! He carried a rust-encrusted trident.

"Are you—" Lasker began.

"Baalzabub. Yes I am. And I have been waiting for you for a long time! Ever since I spoke to your young woman in her dreamtime! You have many questions, and they will be answered. Come to my humble home — along the path — through the doorway, you will see, come." He moved past Lasker and the others slowly, using the rusty trident as a cane, and led them along.

173

"We will have some fowl-pie and good fruit! Come, come. I don't often entertain." He slapped Lasker on the back heartily, too heartily.

As they followed Baalzabub along a shaky, vine-supported plank path, Lasker queried, "You had visitors before?"

"Yes, but not very often. Maybe every few centuries. Some Tibetans came here a few times. I gave them some teachings. One Semitic traveler, an excellent young man named Joshua — *something* — came here, say, oh about two thousand years ago. He had some wounds I had to heal — on his hands. Some Romans, I understand, maltreated him. Nice chappie. He stayed only three days. You think I look young? Clean living does it, chap!"

They soon came upon a tree house, a most excellent and large tree house. Any child would be ecstatic to see such a thing, Lasker thought. He wondered if Baalzabub had constructed it.

They went inside. There was no furniture, nor pictures, or anything, just straw mats. They sat down and their host put down his trident, went in another room, and soon returned with cups of what appeared to be red wine and some of the prunelike fruit. Plus a crock of steaming — *something!* Lasker didn't like the smell, but Rinchen and Tsering took a dollup of the bird-stew and they savored it, chewed it with gusto.

Dorjee, when she reached out for the proffered cup of wine, revealed her missing finger. "Oh? What's that? Missing a finger?" Baalzabub added, "That won't do!"

She started weeping. Lasker, rather annoyed at Baalzabub's inappropriate comment, explained briefly how the finger had come to be removed, by the Communist torturers.

174

"Very nasty people," Baalzabub said. "But no serious damage that can't be undone! Here, child, let me see that hand again. Maybe there's something I can do."

She went closer to him, and Baalzabub held her mutilated hand and looked it over carefully. His red fingernails traced around the wound. "Ah, nice! The infection has been handled well—"

"Thanks to Cheojey's ministrations," Lasker said. "He's a medical lama."

"Medical lama, eh?" the tree-man said. "Well then, he would be interested in this . . ." Baalzabub got up rapidly and motioned for Dorjee and the lama to follow him into the side room, and Lasker invited himself to tag along.

There was a cabinet in the room, a crudely carved doorless box with several shelves—all full of earthen jars with what looked like twigs and herbs in them. Medicines, probably. And there was one glassine jar with a bluish liquid in it.

Baalzabub moved his rather fat lips almost imperceptibly to say, "This will help your finger," and he took down the liquid and popped the cork. "Smell this, Cheojey Lama."

The Tibetan doctor did, and smiled. "A strong medicine, I believe."

"Quite so! It is the essence of a small crustacean creature—a crab, you call them. Now, here, give me your hand, girl." Baalzabub rubbed the compound on Dorjee's missing joint.

"It hurts," she winced. "It feels like fire."

"Only for a while. Watch." He had a devilish glee in his dark eyes.

As they all watched Dorjee's hand, a miraculous thing

175

happened. Slowly, inch by inch, a new finger started to grow. "Oh! How can this be?" Dorjee gasped.

"Crustaceans — such as the river crabs here, and some starfish — grow new limbs easily, when they lose one. It is a substance in their body that enables this process. And my little bottle here contains the blue substance!"

After a while, the finger, including nail, had grown completely. Lasker held her and caressed her tightly. She was overjoyed and ran into the other room to show the others what had happened. Give the devil his due . . .

Lasker looked at Baalzabub with new respect. Then the devil said, "Now you can repay me for this, Lasker."

"What do you want — my soul?"

"No! Just be my guests for a few days," Baalzabub laughed. "We will exchange ideas and information. I will learn something of your surface ways, and you will learn what you need to know."

"Accepted gladly," Lasker said, speaking for everyone, he was sure. "But what do you mean, 'surface ways?' "

"Don't you know?" the chortling "young" man said. "You are under the earth thousands of miles. This is the place called hell."

As they sat in the lofty tree-house room and asked questions of their host, Lasker's party could smell the cookfires of the Indians camped below. Pork. Some had not been lost, and was being cooked. As Baalzabub explained strange and mysterious things about the land they had been in for a week now, the Pukas camped below began playing on their reed pipes. A weird melody that fit the answers Lasker was receiving.

"Where are we, Baalzabub?"

"In a place called Eden, if you wish to call it that." He laughed. "The Tibetans know this place as Shambhala. To many Christians, it is familiar as a place called hell. Suit yourself."

Lasker had never intended to meet the devil. But he had expected, if he did, to find someone rather more evil in appearance and demeanor. "Are you the devil called *Beelzebub?*"

"Quite so. I am Balzabub, but some mispronounce my name. Some call me the devil, and do not think much of me or my domain." With those words, their host pushed back his mat of red hair and revealed two small horns. As Lasker's heart pounded wildly, he laughed more than a little maniacally. "Oh, don't take it so hard! My ornery ways have been much much exaggerated! Now please pronounce *your* names, so I might not mix *them* up, as others have mixed up my name, and sullied my reputation!"

They each told the devil their names. Lasker's voice shook a bit as he did so. Lasker was more upset than the others at this revelation of Baalzabub. So they were in hell, and he was the devil! To the Tibetans, the devil has little meaning. The universe, to the Tibetans, is not divided up into forces of Good and Evil, God and Devil. To Tibetans, all was *samsara* — illusion — so what did it matter?

Seeing the upset look in Lasker's eye, the Hermit gave him a stern glare of warning. It told Lasker to calm down. And he did, as much as possible. Still, when the devil handed Dorjee ripe fruit, and she took a bite and then offered it to Lasker, he hesitated before biting into it. The snake on Baalzabub's shoulders hissed a bit.

177

"Why does the sun not move?" Lasker asked, finally, getting his tongue back.

"Didn't I tell you you were in the bowels of the earth? That is *not* the sun above. You are looking up at the core of the earth. The flaming core is above these eternal clouds. If you wish, later you can climb the ladder behind the house. It is a long climb, but it leads to the very top of the Eden-tree, and there you will be above the clouds and can see for yourselves."

"How can it be that we can be alive here so far under the earth? There should be millions of pounds of pressure here, and molten magma—"

"Well, you see, Lasker, now that you are here, it is obvious that the earth is not designed the way most of your scientists conjectured!" He laughed, drooling a bit. "Sorry, bad teeth."

"How old are you?" Cheojey asked.

"I am 2,666 years old, today," the devil said. "Born in the Flood."

"Happy birthday," Cheojey responded, as they all almost fell back onto the mats.

"Thank you," Baalzabub replied. "And to you all, a Happy New Year."

Lasker was too flabbergasted to go on, and Cheojey picked that up and took over the questioning. He asked, "What is the green rippling in the sky?"

"There *is* an evil here in hell," the devil said. "You must go and stop it. The power reaches to the surface, to the green-robed ones. The world above is threatened by this development. The skull's great power was not always functioning. Something has happened to awaken it." Baalzabub yawned. "It is late. I must help you destroy this evil. And I *will* help you. Tomorrow. We must rest now."

"But there are many more questions!" Lasker protested. But the devil had already laid down and closed his eyes. "He is an old man despite his look," Cheojey said. "We must let him sleep. Have patience."

"Not right now," Lasker said, "I want to climb that ladder and see this earth's core standing still in the sky. I just can't believe it, until I see for myself."

"I'll climb with you," Tsering said. The others preferred to wait.

Lasker and the rebel leader climbed and climbed, the rickety ladder creaking and swaying, barely secured by rotting vines on each branch above. Baalzabub, at his age, apparently had little appetite for repairs. Many times, they thought to turn back, but their curiosity drove them on up. Finally, they broke through the clouds and then the ladder ended in a top branch. And from there they beheld the burning, flaring orange globe in the sky. It was a meteorlike pitted mass that was not the sun, and could only be what Baalzabub had told them: The earth's flaming core! It was so intense and burning that they spent little time up there, and they climbed back down without saying a word. They *were* in hell, that was for *damned* sure!

Most of the party slept in the larger room with the devil. Jade Jaguar didn't seem to need sleep so he sat outside on the plank pathway and did nothing. Maybe he was thinking, Lasker conjectured. Or meditating. Or plotting.

Lasker and Dorjee went into the other room, the one with the medicine cabinet, to lie down. Dorjee wanted to

179

make love, and Lasker did, too. But he felt very uncomfortable at first, holding her in the devil's house! Making love in hell wasn't his lifelong desire. Still, the energies of passion and desire overtook all objections as to place and situation, and they embraced. And began a ritual older than the devil, a ceremony between man and woman as old as time itself . . .

They had a breakfast of more bird-pie and fruit, and some stimulating tealike drink — Baalzabub had used a small crossbow to fire several arrows at birds nearby the window. The birds' bodies were drawn in by a string attached to the arrows. Baalzabub cooked on a small stove he fed leaves and twigs into, in a corner alcove of the room, sitting on a rock. This was not quite the devil that Lasker had been told to fear in Sunday school! But he was not sanguine in the least about the robust tree-man's intentions. *One* of the bad attributes that the devil was supposed to have was *trickiness!*

The questions continued. Lasker asked, "You spoke of an evil that we are supposed to destroy. You said you would help us. What is this thing that makes the green rays?"

"I am sure," Baalzabub replied, "that you have all guessed that the thing that must be destroyed — or at least shut off — is the power source that supplies the green energy to the Bonpo. That energy empowers the crystal skulls that your enemy possess." The devil smiled. "I also see in all your minds that you wonder how I know these things. If you were as old as I, you would develop the other unused parts of your brain, the part that can readily access the universal knowledge held in the akashic record. That source of knowledge beyond time and space is another subject entirely. For now, just believe me. You must head directly to turn off the evil power. You will need complex directions. I shall give them to you, as well as other advice. So you don't get killed there in the great wreckage."

"Great *wreckage?*" Lasker asked. "Of what?"

The devil laughed. "What you seek, dear ones, is a power source that is part of a wrecked interstellar spacecraft! The power that is being transmitted to the Bonpo is coming from the great skull aboard that spacecraft. That skull is a force-field of the interstellar drive-mechanism. It has come *on* recently. And it is still very powerful after all these years."

"This is hard to believe," Lasker said. "If this ship from space exists, why did it suddenly become active?"

"No magic there, Lasker. I believe someone has spoken the access code. The Bonpo, I believe, have uncovered an old inscription on a Cultivator device left near the surface. They have learned to recite its words. It is a code that the ancient mechanism in the ship is programmed to respond to. It is as if a Cultivator was asking the Force-field drive to turn on, and to transmit power."

Lasker heaved a deep breath and asked, "Tell us where it is and what dangers to avoid."

"I can help you understand the spacecraft, and how it has flown here. That is all the help, aside from directions to it, that I can give. Such a great ship of the cosmos doesn't actually *fly* through space, it materializes in *thick* time-space and dematerializes in, er, *thin* time-space . . . there are not words, alas, in any earth-language, to explain fully. But I try this attempt at explaining, because one of you is wondering how the

181

spacecraft could have wound up thousands of miles under the surface."

"I was thinking that," the Hermit admitted. "Your mind-powers are amazing."

"Yes, they are. But they were not always so. Once I was like you, and would have lived a dull, and short, life. Then I stumbled on the wreck. And I put some device on my head in that ship. The thing was some sort of mind-booster. I almost was driven mad, but by the time I got it off my head, I was—different. It made me crazy for a while . . ."

"If you have such powers," Tsering proposed, "then perhaps you could tell us if the Bonpo that were after us are anywhere near."

"Oh, they are near," Baalzabub chuckled. "And they will be here soon, to try to kill you all."

Chapter Nineteen

Rinchen looked around slyly, holding the handle of his sword, ready to draw it out of its scabbard. "Just how soon will the Bonpo be here?"

"Relax, young man," Baalzabub reassured. "They will not arrive for several of your surface days. You will be long gone by the time they come — I will have time enough to tell you about what you need to know — if you are fast learners. You must understand the nature of the great interstellar vessel you will find in the grass valley. Just a few simple concepts before you attempt to enter the great vessel. So come, sit down and listen to me."

As the rain dripped incessantly outside, they sat and listened to the devil expound about many things.

Baalzabub sat cross-legged, his eyes upward as if he were in a trance. His lecture went on for hours, yet it was astonishingly interesting. Lasker was awed at the knowledge he had of the interior design of the spacecraft, and how it worked. He wondered how much of this technical information was getting through to his companions. During the lecture, he looked over at

Dorjee—she seemed enraptured. And Tsering, too, was paying close attention. Even Rinchen, who had no head for technical matters, was listening intently to Baalzabub's elaborate treatise on power sources and interstellar drives, as if it were the most fascinating thing he'd ever heard.

Baalzabub must have them in a spell, Lasker realized. Indeed, Baalzabub's voice sounded distant; it sounded like he was a spirit-medium talking from a great distance. He spoke slowly, and the lecture went on for hours.

Eventually Baalzabub broke off and looked down at the floor and smiled. He dismissed them and told them to have refreshment and then get some sleep.

"I'm surprised," Lasker told Rinchen as they munched on hard sweet fruit and drank the bark tea, "that you found the lecture so interesting. I mean—all that stuff was rather technical."

Rinchen looked puzzled. "Technical? Why, all he did was relate the many adventures of a great hero upon different worlds far beyond the earth. Wonderful tall tales full of fighting and triumphs."

Cheojey looked puzzled. "Adventures? Oh, no. That's not what I heard. Baalzabub spoke about the philosophy of nonbeing and nonarising, a rather complete explanation of the basic Buddhist Emptiness concepts as elaborated in the Abidharma texts. Utterly fascinating."

"Eh, what's this? Are you mad?" Tsering complained. "He did not speak of those things at all. Why, Baalzabub spoke about clan weaponry, the making of great swords, metalurgy, and—"

Dorjee touched her lover's sleeve and smiled, "It is clear that everyone heard something different. That is Baalzabub's way. I, for one, was told a wonderful story about the dream-time before the beginning of the world. A love story."

Rinchen, who disliked anything smacking of the supernatural, looked disturbed. He put down his tea and said, "By what manner of black art is this possible? How could he speak differently to each of us simultaneously?"

"He's the devil," Lasker said.

Cheojey said, "Certain high Buddhist lamas also can do this, Rinchen. Obviously Baalzabub had the knowledge to speak in this multiple way also. I am sure that if we had recorded his words, they would seem to have contained nothing but gibberish. Be thankful that we didn't have to hear what would have been most boring to us. I, for one, would have been very tired to listen to any discussion of weaponry!"

They slept. Dorjee held Lasker in the darkness—in the separate room. "We are alone—to make love."

"Yes," he replied. "But I feel sort of uncomfortable—after all, if Baalzabub is not pulling our legs, we are in the Eden tree, in hell, and we are the guests of someone who in the West is called the devil." But like the "night" before, passion ruled. Lasker soon forgot all worries, lost himself in the sensuousness of her arms.

Their lovemaking was very intense. All Lasker could hear was the rain and Dorjee's low moans. Their lovemaking went on for hours, until they fell deep into sleep.

Rinchen was the first one up, disturbed by the whooshing sound of an arrow. Instantly on his feet, the warrior had his sword at the ready. The noise came from Baazlabub's porch. Rinchen found the door ajar and peered out. Their red-haired host was at his window, reeling in a long string. He had fired an arrow with string attached, from a crossbow that lay on the floor. When the string was drawn into the window, Rinchen saw that a red-plumed bird was impaled upon the barbed arrow. There was going to be more fowl-stew for breakfast!

Rinchen went back to his sleeping pallet, and found Tsering, Cheojey and the Hermit up and stretching. Cheojey had the small stove heating a pot of tea. There was a basket of buns next to it. First course of breakfast.

They sat and ate. Rinchen, spearing a bun with his knife and taking a huge bite, asked, "Shouldn't we awaken Lasker and Dorjee?"

Tsering smiled. "This is their best chance to be alone. They need as much time as possible, to overcome their separation."

"Yes," Cheojey said. "Let them *sleep* a bit longer!"

"Of course, you are right," Richen smiled. "They probably are exhausted from lovemaking. I myself could go on making love for hours without exhaustion. But others—"

"Ha," the Hermit scowled, sipping his too-hot tea gingerly and putting it down, "bragging again?"

Rinchen turned a bit red. Cheojey smoothed over the angry silence by saying, "I know Rinchen has many wenches back in Gyarong Province. They're probably pining over him now."

"More likely," Tsering couldn't help teasing, "they have forgotten all about Rinchen, and are in the arms of other men."

"And how about your wife," Rinchen said in bad humor. "Where is *she* right now?"

"I am a co-husband," Tsering retaliated, referring to the fact that Tibetan women can have two husbands, usually related ones. "Tenpa is safe within my brother's arms, if you must know!"

"Ha!" snickered the Hermit. "He got you with that one!"

Lasker was awakened by the sounds of the others of his party discussing what to eat for breakfast in the adjacent room. He yawned, and after admiring the way her raven hair spilled across the pillow, shook Dorjee awake. They dressed quickly and went in to join their friends. The blinds had been raised—it was raining, *again*.

On this, the second day of their visit to Baalzabub's tree house, they were treated to some massive doses of wild-bird pie. It seemed that the old devil was up all night using his crossbow and the arrows with the lines attached, to spear and bring in their breakfast. Lasker nibbled. Rinchen, for once, ate with gusto—he needed meat most of all. Then they were again called upon to listen to Baalzabub's words.

Lasker learned all about the interstellar drive of the

spacecraft. According to their host, it was a force-field that distorted the time-space fabric itself, creating a contained "black hole." Baalzabub described the device as eight feet high, and shaped like a skull—not a human skull, but a Cultivator's elongated skull. *Why* the Cultivators formed it in this manner was a matter of their artistic preference. The skull, to the Cultivators, was a highly cherished aesthetic form.

"What has all this to do with the Bonpo's new power, and the green flickering in the sky," Lasker interjected.

"Let me explain to you something even more clearly, Lasker. The little crystal skulls that adorn the necklaces of the Bonpo tap that great force-field's power. This is a recent phenomena—something that had been turned off for centuries has somehow become activated. Whether by accident or design, the Bonpos' crystal skulls now are receiving the vast power of the force-field within the spacecraft. The Bonpo know the activating code—one of the mantras that the Bonpo recite. Perhaps they believe it is magic that actually turned on their little devices! They have thought for centuries that the crystal skulls were mere ornaments. They collected them in the mountains. Not knowing that the little skulls are the leftovers of Cultivator-race earth-explorers. The mantrams that the Bonpo speak—derived from an ancient inscription—are a coded sequence of Cultivator syllables to activate the crystal skulls, which receive power from the force-field aboard the spacecraft.

"*Mind power*, Lasker. The *awesome* power that now makes it possible for the Bonpo to take over the world, once they realize its full potential. You must turn off the source of that power—enter the ship and turn it off!

But the danger in the spacecraft for you, Lasker, or anyone who tries to disarm the interstellar drive power source is great. The force-field *bends reality*. You will not be able to do the simplest things if you do not understand that. You must remember that thought is *real*. Thought creates reality. Comprehend?"

"Not at all, Baalzabub, I'm confused," Lasker admitted.

"Good! Always be confused! Never know what you are doing. And that way, you can jump between realities, Lasker. Oh, I know my little talk means nothing to you now. But when you are in the reality-bend near the great skull, you will understand. Jump — jump between realities like a skater jumps over barrels on an icy lake. Don't touch it; disarm it another way. To touch it is death."

Lasker asked, "How do I turn it off, if I don't touch it?"

"I don't know," Baalzabub responded. "I don't know if it *can* be turned off, or what the means of destroying it could be. But one thing: you must understand about reality-tunnels."

The redhead-of-the-great-tree went on to explain the concept of reality tunnels in terms of pure mathematics. It should all have been incomprehensible to Lasker, yet it was as if Baalzabub fed the knowledge *directly* into Lasker's brain! At the end of the lecture, Lasker was nearly overwhelmed. He had received what would have taken years of explanation by ordinary means to understand. He knew how an interstellar drive worked!

Their host looked far away and said, "Once, as I said, I observed the ship. It is shaped like one huge silver disk. I have seen there are many corridors in there — and that there are things inside that are not for me to see. I learned that many centuries would pass until a man — you, Lasker — came along to enter the great ship. That I would guide him. And now it has come to pass. The great meditator who has dreamed the universe into existence has created this drama. All wise and powerful is he."

"*You* speak of *God?*"

Baalzabub smiled, "God? Who said God? Each of us dreams his own dream! But dreams can kill. Be careful inside the great silver disk. I have grown fond of you. I want you to succeed. But I can give you no protection. I can give you no more advice. I will meditate now — when I come out of my trance I will expect you are all gone. Good-bye and good luck!"

The lecture was over!

As they had done after the first lecture, Baalzabub's visitors discussed their impressions of what their host had spoken about.

Cheojey said, "I have learned all the answers to the riddle of Shambhala. Over the centuries wise men have guessed as to the location of the kingdom from where all the knowledge of the Tibetan oversouls had been dispersed. I know now that Shambhala is in many places. This land we are in, one of the continents under the earth, is part of Shambhala. So is the moon. And many caves near the earth's surface! Shambhala is *all* the places that the great starfaring race known as the Cultivators have left their tools, their libraries, their weapons. Shambhala is a federation of many worlds. It is all the areas that the Cultivators ruled, all over the universe once. It is in space, outer and inner. The Cultivators were here under the earth tens of thousands of years ago, and made this land part of Shambhala. They will return from Zod — their native planet — soon, to see what their creation — mankind — has made of itself. The riddle of Shambhala is solved. It is my job to return to the surface and relate this fact to the high lamas — to report it to His Holiness!"

Dorjee said, "I know the direction to the great ship. I can get us there. It is all clear in my mind. You will see."

"That's a relief," Lasker said. "I thought for a while that Baalzabub was withholding that information from us."

"And I," said Rinchen proudly, "have learned something that I have always wondered about. You know how I hate what the Chinese Communists have done to Tibet: The Chinese bury nuclear waste in its soil, chop down its great forests, and ship them to China. You know I hate how mankind has destroyed vast parts of the world. Now I bring a message to all the people. Baalzabub has told me that the earth — above and below — is a living thing. If mankind harms it too much, it will respond and destroy mankind. Mankind fears destroying nature, but that is impossible! However, it is very likely nature will destroy all us surface people, says Baalzabub, if we persist in what we are doing — raping the earth! Polluting. When man destroyed vast areas of the rain forests in Africa, the Earth-mother acted to protect herself. She has produced a great new disease, initially spread by the green monkey, but now spread blood-to-blood among humans. Baalzabub told me that another more horrible and contagious disease will arise from the Amazon forest that humanity is destroying. And eventually all the insects, the sea life, too, will bring us many more diseases, to whittle humanity down to a fraction of its present size. I will deliver this message to those who would hear it. They will listen! They must. Or, by all the boddhisattvas in Tushita heaven. I will *cut them down with my sword!*"

Tsering said he had heard something else entirely, "something very important if we are to accomplish our mission. It is, however, a secret for now." Tsering refused to discuss it. "I will tell you all in good time. I will only say our success, once within the great starship, depends upon it."

The Hermit said, "I have no secret! I learned how to operate the great library devices within the craft. It will be useful in my further studies of the great Cultivator race. Material for many years of meditation in my cave! I *so* long to return to my quiet practices! As for you, my young disciple," the Hermit intoned, turning toward Lasker, "what did you hear in the lecture?"

Lasker said, "A lot. Difficult to explain, I'm afraid. There is a device in the ship. A device that transmits to the Bonpo crystal skulls. The power source within the ship must be disarmed. And the key to doing so is within what I have learned about reality, and thought, and jumping barrels. *Never mind!* I couldn't possible explain all I heard today."

"Again," said the lama, giggling, "Baalzabub's lecture was very good! It is obvious the devil told us each a piece of what we need to know, so that when we reach the great ship, we can accomplish the task."

Chapter Twenty

Lasker said, "Our host has rather abruptly withdrawn his invitation to partake of his hospitality. The Bonpo are coming and that means we'd better pack up and leave."

Tsering shrugged. "I for one am willing to leave here, right now. But we must take along the crossbow; Baalzabub said to me that we would need it — and also the arrows."

"For protection?" Rinchen snarled, "Why, I can provide all the protection needed."

"Yes, I understand that," Tsering agreed heading off the inevitable argument. "But our host wants me to take the crossbow," Tsering insisted. "I think we should follow his desire in this matter. As I will carry the crossbow, so you will be the swordsman for us all."

That seemed to assuage the giant warrior.

Cheojey, always concerned for the welfare of others, interjected, "But he uses it to provide himself food. What is Baalzabub to hunt with?"

Tsering said, "I'm sure he'll make out. Baalzabub

insists we take it along. If we are to trust all he has told us, then we should trust his advice on this as well — it is a small matter."

"Take it along, then, Tsering," the Hermit snapped impatiently. "Far better *that* than endless discussion." He looked out at the shak branches that led to the elevator platform. "I'm sure our time will be better spent figuring out how to get back down without falling."

That comment seemed to send Dorjee into a reverie. Her eyes rolled up and she recited: "When we descend, we must fend for ourselves." Dorjee spoke in some sort of poetic meter. She almost sang the words, like a song.

"Dorjee?" Lasker asked. "Are you all right?"

Her eyes fluttered and she smiled, "Oh, did I say something? Oh, yes. The directions and omens that I have been given are not in my conscious mind. They are in my deep-brain, and have to be said like a song. Do you want me to sing the song so that we might find our way?"

"Directions are fine, but what do you mean," asked Tsering, coming close to her, "by those words, 'we must fend for ourselves?' "

"I honestly don't know." Dorjee looked truly perplexed.

Tsering slung the crossbow over his shoulder and likewise the quiver of sharp arrows. They all packed their gear and left. In the drizzle, cascading monkeys all around them, raucous birds serenading their every step, they left Baalzabub's domain. Lasker's last glance at the devil through the window showed he was still sitting down, meditating peacefully. Not exactly the big-bad-wolf devil Lasker had heard so much about all his life!

They reached the platform elevator and looked for a lever. "Maybe I can help," Jade Jaguar said. He spoke so seldom that his soft voice started them.

"Be our guest," Lasker said, intrigued. This was the first time the high priest had volunteered.

Jade Jaguar calmly studied the lift mechanism. Then without further words, he started to work the wooden levers, to operate the rather complex descent controls. A series of pegs, when displaced, released different gears on the platform. The Indian high priest slowly lowered them on the long vine rope, without a jerk.

During the long, slow descent, Tsering seemed to be very involved with playing with his new toy, the crossbow. To Lasker's annoyance—why it should annoy him he knew not—the rebel leader kept nocking an arrow and pulling the string taut—as if sighting some imaginary enemy. But, of course, Tsering didn't fire.

They were swaying back and forth a lot as they descended from the tree canopy, so much so that the Hermit called out for someone below to please come and steady the ladder. No one did that. When they reached the surface, they found that no one else was there. No supplies, and no Indians. The Puka Indians had all melted away into the jungle.

They all looked at Jade Jaguar. "Did you know they were leaving?"

"No, I didn't. Maybe they are still within earshot. Hold on a moment." Jade Jaguar cupped his hands to his mouth and called out a cry of ululating syllables.

No reply.

"Be on guard," whispered the rebel chief, taking out his clan-sword, "they may have been attacked by the Bonpo."

They had found out what Dorjee's words meant when she recited the words, "We must fend for ourselves." They spread out and confirmed that Lasker's initial reaction was quite correct. There was no sign of struggle — even after Rinchen inspected the ground, sniffing it for enemy spoor!

Jade Jaguar said, "I cannot understand it. They left without my permission."

Lasker wondered if the sub-chief might be pulling a coup at this opportune moment. Jade Jaguar said, "I will find them."

"You may come along with us, if you wish," Lasker stated. "I don't think you have any choice, unless you can make it back to the village alone. They are all long gone."

Jade Jaguar smiled his green-toothed best. "It is my honor to go with the gods."

Lasker stepped a foot or two, and then scratched his head. "Which way, Dorjee?"

Her eyes rolled up. Lasker didn't like how pale she got when she did this. She sang out, "Follow the stream to the north, just as all life must return to its source. We must go farther than the reeds wish to grow. After the brook, then a ruin of ancient times, blocks the rapids . . ." she faded out. Cheojey was smart. He was writing down her words.

"What else, Dorjee?"

She swayed a bit, and then added, "The rapids turn sharply like a knife, and where it does, there is the source of the life-water. Water comes from rocks, and goes where it will."

"What the hell is she saying?" Tsering asked.

"I think she means," snorted the Hermit, "we go along *that* brook, and then we will be heading straight. Don't worry. When the mist rises, there will be no need for further songs. We will again see the green fluctuations in the air."

But Dorjee said, "Five thousand times the length of a swamp reed, we seekers will come to the clearing of red grass. In the middle of that clearing is the great wreck itself."

Lasker whispered, "Cheojey, got all that?"

The lama smiled. "Yes. I think so." He put away his pad. "Catch her."

"Huh?" Then Lasker saw Dorjee was wavering on her feet. He caught her before she fell over. "Did I tell you? Do we know where to go?" she asked.

"You did fine. Thanks."

Without another word, they set off as indicated, along a small brook.

"What about food?" Rinchen mumbled. They had been walking for hours. "We haven't even reached the rapids Dorjee spoke of yet. Perhaps we are lost. What do we eat?"

Lasker said, "I am sure Tsering's crossbow can hit small animals or birds. We have your flintbag to make a fire to cook. We know—thanks to Jade Jaguar—what is edible of the vegetation. Don't worry."

"If you wish not to *create* food, I can find food," Jade Jaguar confirmed. "But I cannot understand why we do everything the hard, Puka way."

They didn't know what to say, but the lama had a reply that seemed to satisfy the high priest. "Ah, we gods are *enjoying* ourselves pretending to be human. So we must go *all the way.*"

Onward they tread, and finally Dorjee said, "Look! Rapids. And the ruin."

It was the ruin, Lasker decided, of an ancient water wheel and adjoining house. A medieval structure.

"Here the rapids are contained—by the old spillway," Dorjee said proudly. "Trust me."

"I trust *you,*" Rinchen said. "It's the old man Baalzabub I don't trust."

"What choice do we have except to trust him," the Hermit scowled. "Neither Cheojey nor I have any psychic powers, or any of our other powers here. I can't even make a rain cloud, so we must go by his guidance."

So they continued along, followed the water, as Dorjee's poetic words indicated.

Lasker, from time to time, had to steady his lover. She walked with strength, but her balance seemed off, even on smooth, level ground. He was worried about Dorjee. Ever since the dream-ordeal, she hadn't seemed to be *quite*—sane. That faraway look in her eyes disturbed him. When would she snap out of it?

"I am all right," she said, interpreting his look. "It's just that the images that have been in my mind, particularly the after-images of the world of the dream-time, are so powerful! I sometimes slip into a reverie." Dorjee gave him a smile that melted away his

198

dark thoughts. "Don't worry, I am — basically — all right!"

It was that qualifier, "basically" that worried Lasker!

Chapter Twenty-one

The much smaller party traveled onward with rapidity, following Dorjee's singsong trance directions.

"It is good to be among gods," Jade Jaguar said, out of nowhere, as they trekked across a rolling plain dotted with red bushes. "When traveling to where none have gone before, one needs to be with gods. I would not do this thing without divine protection."

Lasker, wondering if there was a hint of mockery in the Indian's tone, asked, "What would have worried you if we *weren't* gods?"

"Why, as you know, there are creatures here in the Beastlands. According to legend, there are killer-beasts that dwarf the great anacondas of the waters. And insects the size of wild boars."

"Great," Lasker moaned, almost inaudibly. Still, Baalzabub hadn't mentioned any such danger. Hopefully such beasts were truly just legends!

They continued to wend their way north along the waters toward their goal. Once or twice they sighted a slithery huge snake on an overhanging branch, or a few raucous monkeys. But there were no giant menaces. Lasker was about to relax, when all hell broke loose.

Shrieking sky-menaces swooped down at them. Huge *bats* coming in low and fast, like fighter planes. "Watch out," Lasker cried, being the first to spot them. "Lie flat!"

They barely had time to do what he shouted when pairs of knife-sharp talons swept by, mercifully just missing catching any bare throats. The bats, annoyed, shrieked out.

"Tsering! Shoot the arrows, Tsering," Lasker yelled as he rose up enough to see that the ten-foot wing-spanned creatures of hell were wheeling on the horizon, coming in for another run at them!

As the bats shrieked out their demonic challenge, Tsering ignored Lasker's shouted plea. The rebel-chieftain put the devil's crossbow down and instead took up his clan sword.

He held it close to his body, ran to the left. The bigger bat veered and, drooling saliva, came straight at the one-eyed hero. At the last second, Tsering spun about on his heels and jabbed out, skewering the thing! The bat had such velocity that it lifted Tsering off the ground for a dozen feet, before falling dead atop him, covering the warrior in red, sticky blood.

The other bat sent out a wail of despair. It sounded like despair, anyway, and then flapping wildly, as if in a rage, made a short turn and came around to avenge its mate.

But as it approached, the Indian stood up to his full seven feet and quickly raised the short tube of his blow-gun. He inserted a dart, and put the tube to his mouth.

PHHHOOOOT! The dart flew out and struck the

rapidly approaching bat's face between the eyes. The bat flailed wildly and dropped. It skidded on the ground to come face to face with Lasker. He stared for a millisecond into the slavering, still-dripping jaws, and then rolled to the side. "Jeez, what a shot!"

The rebel leader threw off his skewered bat and came to lift Lasker. "Are you hurt?"

"No. Thanks to the Indian's aim, I'm not."

Jade Jaguar was standing over the thing he had killed, and he now bent to remove and wipe the dart off on his sleeve, and then repocket it.

They sat around for a while watching the sky. There were no more comers. Lasker finally asked Tsering, "Why didn't you use the crossbow?"

"Didn't have time," Tsering said. Lasker nodded. But Tsering *had* time enough. Why didn't he use the crossbow?

As they traveled onward, always with an uneasy eye to the clouds above, Lasker was more uneasy than ever. Dorjee wasn't the only one of the party who was acting strangely now. Tsering had a great secret, and Jade Jaguar was becoming ever more powerful a figure, and ever more enigmatic.

They camped out in a clearing and took turns on guard duty. Lasker asked to examine the crossbow, but Tsering demurred.

Jade Jaguar, on Rinchen's insistence, went into the brush and soon had scrounged up some jungle food. He had gathered thick, juicy, edible leaves and some bamboolike reeds. Then they built a small fire and cooked them. Singed, the reeds were tasty enough, and nutritious, but Rinchen wanted meat. "Another time, friend," Lasker promised, "I'll buy you a six-inch-thick

203

steak. For the celebration when we get home."

While they ate second portions, Dorjee kept nodding off. Which made Lasker realize that they hadn't slept for a long long time. It might have been two days of travel since the tree house. As it started to drizzle, he said, "We need shelter, and sleep."

"I can make a shelter," Jade Jaguar offered, "if you do not wish to create one out of thin air." Again that mocking tone.

"Then do so," Lasker ordered. Soon, having gathered abundant vines, the priest constructed a lean-to big enough for all. With clumps of the soft grass as bedding, they had a decent place to rest. The thatched roof of leaves was well waterproofed. They slept well. All except Lasker. He was restless, he said, and so he therefore took the first watch. He sat on a boulder ten feet from the lean-to, watching and waiting for who knows what. Tsering, he noted, was sleeping with the crossbow and quiver in his arms like it was a prized maiden. Were they all to go mad, one by one?

As he listened to Rinchen snoring, Lasker leaned back against a tree and thought about their journey so far. What really were their chances of success? If there were more giant beasts hereabouts, their weapons were inadequate. The poison-needle blowgun and the swords wouldn't account for much if a squadron of those huge bats should attack. And if the Bonpo search party found and confronted them—they'd be finished. Cheojey and the Hermit indeed had little of their extraordinary powers down here in the bowels of the earth—perhaps because of the green, flickering rays.

Lasker caught himself dozing off. He glanced at the

primitive time device. The twelve-hour glass that was the Indian way of reckoning time had nearly run out. It was Rinchen's turn to stand watch. Good. No way was he going to try to sleep with the big man snoring like that! Lasker had always slept lightly! He yawned and headed back toward the lean-to.

He tapped Rinchen awake and, after the man staggered out to guard duty, Lasker snuggled down close to Dorjee. She gave him a kiss and then her eyes closed again. The poor woman was beyond exhaustion. But her stamina was good. She wouldn't be the first to fall. Lasker worried more about the Hermit. And Cheojey. They were both old. He looked over at them. They seemed so frail when asleep. Just old skin and bones. It seemed that both men breathed very shallowly. He lay on his back, yet Lasker couldn't quite sleep. So he stared up at the ceiling of fronds. Too *light*. He'd never get used to there being no night, no stars. So this was hell . . .

Eventually he did fall asleep.

The Hermit poked him awake with his knobby walking stick. Lasker, grumpy as could be, rubbed his eyes and packed up his gourd of water and parka, which served as a pillow mostly.

Tsering told him, "Bart, we should move on as fast as possible."

Lasker yawned, nodded. Dorjee was already up. She smiled, but it was again that dreamy otherworldly smile. It had stopped raining, but the air was clammy with humidity. He still felt half smothered in the damned lack of sky above. The lack of dark would soon drive him crazy. He only had one desire now—to find the way to get back to the surface. And yet, they must go on and destroy the power source of the Bonpo.

The devil had failed to mention the bats. What else had he not mentioned? What, of all the things Baalzabub said, could be trusted? Lasker didn't like depending on others, especially the devil!

They broke the lean-to down and scattered its parts. No sense in leaving a trail. And they moved onward. Early that "day" they came upon the source of the stream in the rocks. And then they headed through the jungle, as Dorjee directed. Within a few hundred yards, as she promised, they reached the grassy clearing. Lasker, who was in the lead, parted a tangle of ferns with his bowie knife and saw the waving red grass.

And there was an object in the middle of that clearing—a huge silver disk set at an angle into the ground. He exclaimed, "It must be a *mile* in length!"

Nothing that Baalzabub had said prepared him for its sheer size. The full immensity of the ship from space was apparent now. It was the size of a football stadium! No doubt about it, they had reached the Cultivators' wrecked spacecraft. It was in the middle of the wide circular clearing, angled down into it.

They went on without speaking a word, walking rapidly toward the silvery craft. When they came closer it was apparent to Lasker that his first impression of a largely undamaged disk was in error. It had several gaping holes, large enough for a man to easily walk through, in its skin. And the metal seemed bent in several other places. "Why isn't this overgrown with jungle?" Tsering asked Lasker.

"Maybe the energy waves are like radiation. Let's hope it's radiation of a kind not dangerous except by long exposure."

The Hermit summed up all their feelings by saying, "The Cultivators' civilization must be thousands of years beyond ours."

Dorjee touched the metal. And quickly withdrew her slender hand. "What is it made of? It feels warm and soft."

Lasker touched the silvery surface. And he replied, "I don't know. Some sort of alien metal that looks like chrome but isn't."

"Well," the Hermit said impatiently. "Let's see what's inside this crate. There's a hole near the surface—come!" The Hermit was scurrying off a dozen paces ahead and he popped inside the gaping hole. His hand jutted out, "Come—see!" The arm disappeared and they heard hollow metallic footsteps.

Lasker rushed over and he peered inside.

"What do you see?" Dorjee asked, coming up alongside Lasker.

"Nothing. The Hermit must have gone on ahead. It's very dark, but I see some glows here and there. We won't need the crystal light."

One by one they went inside. As their eyes adjusted to the dim light—glowing globes of pale blue along the side of the ceiling—they saw they were in a twisting corridor. A voice ahead echoed, "Come on!" It was the Hermit. They heard footfalls and soon saw his scrawny figure ahead, waving them on. "Come on!" the Hermit repeated impatiently. "Why do we hurry all the way here and now tarry?"

Lasker agreed, in angry tones. "So who's stalling. Stop talking and lead on." The "Holy Terror" did so. The corridor went on for fifty feet, then they came to a fork. Two corridors.

"Which one?" asked the Hermit.

"The one to the left," Lasker said, "toward the center of the ship. The skull, actually a force-field generator, is in the center, according to the words of Baalzabub."

They started down the left tunnel. Soon the going was difficult. They had to step over broken wires and pieces of plastic-looking pipe. "Someone has been in here, breaking things," Rinchen concluded.

"Maybe it was the impact of the crash," the medical lama suggested, "and not intruders."

"Bah," the Hermit mocked, knocking down pieces of broken metal with his knobby walking stick. "Age breaks things down!"

Just then, Dorjee gasped. Lasker turned toward her and saw that her hair was all frizzed out. "Your hair," she smiled, "is sticking out. It's very funny."

Indeed, Lasker noted, *everyone's* hair sort of frizzed out, like they had permanent waves!

"What is doing this?" Rinchen asked. The Tibetan strongman tried to pat down his hair, but it kept rising again.

Lasker stated, "There's powerful electro-magnetic fields here. Shouldn't be dangerous, though."

"How do you know," Rinchen asked, "that it's not spirits doing this?"

"Baalzabub told me there were no dangerous beings in here. Only near the power source is there any real

208

danger from the force-field."

"So he says," Rinchen snorted, unconvinced.

They pressed onward. The tunnel curved like the inside of a snail shell. This continued for a hundred yards. "I suppose if this curving continues, we'll be going deeper and deeper into the ship." Lasker had to admit that he was puzzled, for there were still no signs of any door or any compartments, just bare walls. Where was the crew's quarters, or control room?

"Yes. Why is it so empty?" Rinchen agreed, his deep bass voice echoing down the corridor. "If this is a flying machine, where are the seats? Where are all the motors and things that airplanes have?"

Tsering snapped, "There will be a room for the crew. But it doesn't have motors like a goddamned airplane! Who knows how it is propelled to be able to voyage for a thousand years or more between stars."

"Perhaps we should recite some prayers," Cheojey offered. "Seek the protection of the gods, and their *calmness.*"

"That's a good idea," Tsering said. They went on walking, slowly murmuring along, all reciting the mantra that Cheojey led.

Finally they came to an area of the gray corridor that had a doorway and they went in. It was a room triangular in shape. In it were many devices, some flickering with lights. Geometrically perfect crystal cubes lay in rows on shelves everywhere.

"The control room, for sure," Tsering said. He started to examine the writing on several of the gray boxlike devices.

"I doubt it," Lasker said. "A control room would need some sort of sky-viewing screen. This is just a storage area."

"I think," said the Hermit, picking up a device much like a headphone, "that we have found a treasure. We have found the *library*."

"Where are the books?" Rinchen asked, looking gloomily around.

"Not like a human library, silly," the Hermit snapped. "This place is like libraries I found in several caves beneath Tibet."

The Hermit handed a headphonelike device to Lasker. "You know how to use these! You get up on that platform and put this on, and I'll put one of these little crystal cubes in this device here! Now we will see what we can access."

Lasker groused about "being ordered around," but complied.

As they all stood around, Lasker sat down on the boxy platform. It was soft and giving, quite comfortable despite its metallic appearance. He put the headset on. There was no cord.

"Ready." He closed his eyes.

The Hermit dropped a cube into the device below.

Immediately Lasker felt the room slipping away. And he was *in space*. He was being propelled into outer space! He was riding in the alien craft, going a million miles an hour. No, it was just an illusion, like a TV set, only more complete!

"You okay?" came the Hermit's voice.

"Yes," Lasker said, "but the moon just passed by. This is fantastic! I am sitting in a spacecraft watching the stars crawl by — yet I can talk to you here. Wow, this is much more than a movie. I'm traveling very fast, and there's a planet ahead."

"What's it look like?" the Hermit asked. "Is it blue and red?"

"No! Just passed it! I think it was Saturn. Lots of rings! Oh! The whole starfield ahead just winked out! What a drag!"

"That's because I'm changing the recording," the Hermit said. "I'm not looking to give you a fun time; I'm looking for a special cube. A record of the layout of what's in this ship. Ah, yes. I found the one I'm looking for. Here. How about this one?"

Lasker gasped, and he almost tore the headphones off. "God, there are all these *Cultivators* around me. I'm still in the space ship—upstairs somewhere. Yes, *this* is the control room. Wow—I can understand what they're saying! They don't see me. One of them is telling the other . . ." Then Lasker muttered, *"Hvoorsh wert-lekneb?"* And then Lasker grew silent for a long time.

The Hermit took out the cube. "Well?"

Taking off the headphones, Lasker shook his head. "Well, now I know the layout. The alien described the layout, and what tunnels to take to the bulkhead where the great skull is. Just because I asked him! With this device on, I can speak Cultivatorese! Say, Hermit, this is wonderful . . . Can't I just stay here a while and—"

"No!" said the Hermit. "You are being sucked in; becoming a couch potato! We have found out what we want!" He pulled the headphones away from Lasker, who groaned out, "I guess you're right, Hermit. It's very seductive. More than TV football!"

"Okay, let's go," the Hermit ordered. "Remember what you were told. Remember how to get to the power-source, for the fate of the world is in our

211

hands." When they turned to leave, Jade Jaguar went last — and his hand reached out as he left the library and he flicked off the lights!

Chapter Twenty-two

Following Lasker's lead, taking alternative left and right corridors, they continued along the spiral passage. The party came upon something wholly unexpected: a small chamber set to the side of the corridor, just big enough for the eight-foot-long box it contained. The marblelike box was up on a platform.

"A coffin!" Rinchen gasped, stepping back. "And, its lid is open!"

"It's more like a sarcophagi," Lasker said in hushed tones. He stepped forward to examine it. "It's carved out of some sort of stone, big enough to hold a Cultivator, for sure."

The glassine sarcophagi cover, which was half up, had a wide crack in it. Lasker opened it wide, and peered down into the interior. "Relax, Rinchen," he said after playing the light down inside. "It's empty, except for a bit of dust in the bottom. I think that dust is all that remains of its occupant."

"Why is a coffin here at all," asked Tsering.

Lasker said, "I came across this sort of thing once before. It's not a coffin, it's a 'suspended animation' chamber. A way to sleep for centuries, and awaken alive. The Cultivators use this sort of thing in their spaceships."

"How do you know this?" Rinchen asked in awe.

Lasker smiled, and replied, "I came across the same boxes in a cave in northern Tibet, a few years back."

Cheojey now peered down into the long stone box and rubbed some of the dust inside between his fingers. "If this was a body, it was not a human one. The dust is too heavy. Why do you suppose the alien was lying here in this room alone?"

Lasker thought for a second and answered, "I think he might have been a guard. We're pretty close to the most important part of the ship—the power-source. Something fell on the poor guy's life-chamber, destroying the mechanism that was supposed to preserve his body. And there's only dust left."

Lasker took the little crystal flashlight from Cheojey's hand and he bent inside the stone box and further examined the box's walls. He found a bulbous glass bump. Following his hunch, he reached under the "coffin's" edge, and felt a wire going from the box into the flooring. He pointed these things out, concluding, "This Guardian was wired to receive an alarm, and awaken if unauthorized guests entered the area of the power-field."

"That is correct," Jade Jaguar said.

"How do you know?" Tsering asked, looking at the Indian with narrowed eyes.

"Obvious," the high priest said. "What else would it be, if the Chief God Lasker says it is thus?" Again, there was the hint of a mocking tone to his words.

"Come on," Lasker motioned. "Let's get the job

done."

They went on for another hundred yards until Lasker heard a low hum that indicated to him they were near the final curl of the corridor. At his insistence, they moved single file now. He had a bad feeling about this place. His Mystic Rebel instincts were firing wildly.

When they reached the bulkhead at the end of the corridor, the hum had become a throbbing vibration, intense, like a heartbeat. Like a strangely rhythmed, alien heartbeat.

"Okay," Lasker whispered, though as far as he knew there was no need to whisper, "we're here. And there's no way to get in. See those dots up near the ceiling? I think they're remote sensors, to give warning if anyone violated this holy-of-holies. But the Guardian is long dead, so we can ignore those." Lasker took out his last sphere-bomb, and asked Tsering for his. He put them against the bulkhead.

"What are you going to do?" Dorjee asked, alarm in her voice.

"Blow a hole in the wall. I'll twist the hemispheres of the sphere-bombs as far as they go. The Hermit figured out the more you twist 'em, the longer you have before an explosion. The pair should do the trick. Soon as I set them to go off, we go back down the corridor, fast. The explosion will remove the bulkhead, without touching the force-field. The skull is about three yards inside, in the middle of a circular room. I know where it is from the recording I accessed in the library. I saw the whole layout of this ship, in a flash."

"You sure this is a good idea?" Cheojey asked.

"I have a feeling we don't have a lot of time to pull this off," Lasker frowned. "I want to expose the skull force-field quick, and then find a cut-off device, pull it, and get the hell out of here."

"Good idea," Rinchen said. "Let us be away from this strange silver beast and its heartbeat."

The Hermit was gleeful. "I can't wait to get a look."

Lasker twisted the globular charges and put them back down against the gray-walled bulkhead. They all sprinted away down the corridor like quarterbacks in the Super Bowl. Except for long-legged Jade Jaguar, who just strolled to safety.

They went around the bend of the corridor, out of direct line from the bulkhead. The explosion went off—a loud WHUMPP that popped Lasker's ears. The explosives were silent, but the sound of air rushing in to fill the empty space they created made the noise.

"Okay," Lasker said. "That should have done it. I hope so. Now let's go see."

They were turning the bend when suddenly there was a green glow. And then a hissing, swirling mass of fog. From out of that miasma of green mist emerged Zompahlok, and several of the Bonpo assassins. Zompahlok held up the crystal skull with the glowing green eyes, and Lasker's heart sunk. "Yes, it is I, Lasker. We beat you here, and now the game is over. I knew you would head for the source of our new power. We got here first, because we did not need to seek guidance to find this spacecraft. You see, my crystal skull's eyes, when not in use, always face the great power source! Now Lasker, you are doomed. You will look at the skull . . . *Look at the crystal*

216

skull I hold!"

He tried, but it was useless. Lasker couldn't drag his eyes from the green, swirling rays. As his friends, paralyzed by the green mists, stood frozen in space-time, the rays surged into Lasker's brain, burning at his synapses, invading the core of his very being.

"You will give up this personality of Lasker," Zompahlok intoned. "You will be our champion Raspahloh once more. So close to the power source, the skull is all-powerful. You feel yourself fading, don't you, Lasker?"

Lasker moaned. It was true. He felt all his defenses collapsing. He tried to shout a protective chant, but it only came out as drool. The Yeshe Tsogyal amulet about his neck flickered blue, but sent no counter-ray forth. Already his body posture was changing. As every atom of his mind and body screamed, Lasker was beginning the transformation. He shifted his weight, stooped over. His jaw slackened, and from it trailed a bit of spittle. His expression changed; his lips became twisted with an evil rage. He was succumbing, becoming Raspahloh!

"I am Raspahloh," he said, after a set of tremors seized his body. But deep inside, a human being that could no longer control his own body still screamed, "No! I still live!"

Raspahloh spoke, using the voicebox of the Mystic Rebel in a peculiar way. He spoke in a rasping, low voice, a voice long unused. Raspahloh conversed in the ancient form of Tibetan, as the Bonpo were wont to do. "I have been held a prisoner in Lasker's body for too long," he uttered. "I will have vengeance! I long to serve the Bonpo cause!"

217

Zompahlok smiled, and he lowered the crystal skull. The rays from the skull-eyes faded, like slowing electric pinwheels. "If you *are* Raspahloh," Zompahlok ordered, "then prove it. Seek your vengeance now. Kill Lasker's friends. Do it *now.*"

Chapter Twenty-three

Raspahloh was about to kill everyone in Lasker's group. But he paused in midstride when the Bonpo sorcerer's green slit cat-eyes moved away from him. Zompahlok's eyes had focused on something behind Raspahloh. Danger.

Raspahloh twisted about and beheld someone moving, despite the Bonpo immobility-spell.

It was the Indian! Jade Jaguar was walking slowly forward, unimpeded by the Bonpo magic. He stood his full eight-foot height, overpowering in his noble presence. He uttered words that had a strange portent implicit in them: "Your petty manipulations have no power over me, sorcerers. I am the Guardian. I am a Cultivator. I have regained my memory. My mission is to protect the great power of this ship from being misused. You Bonpo have used the transmitted power of the Great Skull for evil purposes. You wish to conquer this world, to usurp the natural order of events that we Cultivators have set up in ancient days. This *will not be!* You will release Lasker, and depart, *now!*"

Zompahlok didn't answer verbally. Instead he motioned Raspahloh to move against the Guardian. But the minute Raspahloh tried to move, he was rooted to the floor. Seeing this, Zompahlok sent a pair of his assassin henchmen out against the Guardian, with another wave of his hand.

The space-being had discarded his fleshlike gloves, revealing his suction-cup-tipped fingers. His reach was long, and before the assassins touched him, Jade Jaguar had raised both hands and thrust them forward. His cold fingers touched their skulls, and the Bonpo pair burst into green flames, fell on the metal flooring and quickly disintegrated.

Zompahlok raised the crystal skull he held and pointed it at the Guardian. Its green rays inundated the alien without effect. Jade Jaguar produced a small gray tube from within his tunic and pointed it at Zompahlok, and the Bonpo who still remained. Jade Jaguar pressed on the device. A blue ray shot out from the tube, and when it reached the High Sorcerer of Evil and his companions, they glowed red for a second, and then faded away, screaming.

"That takes care of all but one thing," Jade Jaguar intoned, turning toward Raspahloh. "Lasker, if there is any part of you within Raspahloh that is yet alive, it is up to your friend to revive you."

And with those words the jade-toothed being waved his glow-tube over Raspahloh and Lasker's friend Tsering. They both instantly became animate. With a quick smile and wave, the Guardian walked away down the corridor in long quick steps.

Tsering didn't understand what had just happened. One second he had been behind his friend Lasker, heading toward the bulkhead after the explosion, and the next second, Lasker was turned at him, and snarling in a rage. Then he understood. "Oh, no! The transformation," Tsering gasped, "has occurred. You are not Lasker, you are—"

"Yes, I am Raspahloh," the crouched opponent snarled. "I do not understand all that has happened, either. I only know that you and all your companions must die."

Tsering shouted, "Bart! Snap out of it! OM MANI PADME HUM!"

"Better I snap your neck!" Raspahloh hissed, clawing the air in anticipation of tearing the rebel-leader's throat.

Tsering gulped hard, but stood his ground. Baalzabub had warned him to expect the transformation of Lasker at anytime. And the red-headed tree-man had also provided the means of neutralizing Raspahloh and restoring Lasker: the crossbow. But Tsering had let his guard down. They had been so close to finishing up their task, the rebel chieftain had let himself become off guard. In the instant after the charge went off, everything had gone blurry. Now the transformation had occurred, and the only defense, Baalzabub's crossbow, was still slung about Tsering's shoulders. No time to raise it and nock an arrow in its string!

Tsering might have hesitated anyway, for he was supposed to fire the gold-tipped arrow straight into his friend Lasker's heart! Baalzabub had promised that the arrow wouldn't kill Lasker, but that seemed

221

unlikely.

It was all a moot point, however. For now Raspahloh screamed out a blood-oath, leapt into the air to close the distance between them. The rebel leader was able to dodge the thrust only because Raspahloh slipped upon some metal fragments on the floor.

As Raspahloh flew past him, Tsering delivered what would have been a decisive knockout blow to any normal opponent: a forceful, double-hand chop to the back of the fiend's neck. The champion of the Bonpo who possessed Lasker's formidable body took the blow without any apparent ill effect. Raspahloh rolled out of his plunge, and he counter-struck. This time Tsering could not avoid being hit. It was a direct fist-blow delivered at the area of the neck just below the medulla. An E-Kung blow that Lasker had taught to Tsering personally, a year earlier. Luckily, Lasker had *also* taught Tsering the counter-move!

Tsering knew how to twist away from the blow to avoid receiving its full impact and having his spine shattered. But this was his last chance, and he knew it. Tsering had a disadvantage. He had to disable his friend's body, not kill it. He pulled his sword from its scabbard and swung it at Raspahloh's knees. But he struck with the side of the sword, hoping to disable the Bonpo champion without doing permanent damage to the body it used.

A sneering red-eyed Raspahloh was ready. He blocked the sword-blow with a raised knee. Then, smirking in triumph, Raspahloh grabbed Tsering's wrist and squeezed until the man hollered and let go of the weapon's hilt. The sword clattered to the floor. Tsering would die, now, that was for certain. They both sensed it.

But then the others started unfreezing, Rinchen first. The strongman took in the situation quickly: Someone half-blocked from Rinchen's view by a disarmed Tsering was about to kill the rebel leader. Instantly, Rinchen threw himself forward, pulling his sword. He shoved Tsering to safety and jabbed at the unknown opponent with deadly intent. Rinchen had gone for the kill, not knowing until he struck that it was Raspahloh that Tsering was fighting. He would have easily opened his friend Lasker's body with his accurate sword-thrust. But Raspahloh was no ordinary opponent. The deadly move was parried, and Raspahloh delivered a double-fisted smash at Rinchen's lantern jaw.

Cheojey unfroze. And he whipped out his weapon of choice—the flywhisk given to him a few years earlier by the chief fighter in a lost Buddhist outpost. The lama understood what was happenning. As Rinchen fell to the side, stunned, Cheojey faced off against the formidable Bonpo champ. This didn't disturb Raspahloh at all—one old man in tattered robe versus a killer of all killers! But as Raspahloh stepped forward on the attack with his glinting sword, Cheojey suddenly went into action. The flywhisk's many seemingly ineffective rope strands caught the Bonpo champ's sword and jerked it to the side, away from the lama's spry body. Tsering bounded to his feet, and as Raspahloh sought to extricate his blade from the maddening tangle of flywhisk-tendrils, the rebel leader attacked. He drop-kicked Raspahloh with his mighty thewed legs, sending the Bonpo madman sprawling. The sword slipped from the tangle.

Cheojey took the opportunity to bang Raspahloh hard on the right temple, a numbing blow expertly delivered with the butt of the flywhisk. The hit was meant to knock Raspahloh out cold but merely stunned him.

Dorjee, released from her spell, screamed and shouted for Cheojey to stop what he was doing, not understanding that Lasker was no longer the man she knew and loved.

Raspahloh staggered to his feet. It took a second for the cobwebs to start to clear. Too long! The Hermit came out of his statuelike position at this moment, and he came forth lifting his gnarled hickory walking staff up. With great force, he delivered it down on Raspahloh's noggin, and staggered the Bonpo champion.

Tsering, during all of this, managed to nock the gold-tipped arrow into the crossbow. "Step aside," he yelled to the others. Tsering drew the string back and fired the arrow right into Raspahloh's chest, where it went in deep. Raspahloh's cruel eyes went wide and he reeled; his knees sagged. Dorjee cried out from seeing the man she loved receiving such a decisive death-strike. The battle was over. Raspahloh toppled to the flooring, gasping for air.

If it were any other enemy than Raspahloh, now would have been the ideal time to finish him off. Tsering could have easily delivered another arrow on the mark. His sword could have chopped through Raspahloh's neck. But that would have

224

killed Lasker as well as Raspahloh.

Rinchen didn't understand why Tsering had used apparently deadly force. The Tibetan strongman yelled at his friend Tsering just one word: "Why?"

Tsering rapidly explained about the—alleged—power of the arrow, as Raspahloh-Lasker lay sprawled on the floor.

Cheojey confirmed the story. "Baalzabub also informed *me* about the coming transformation of Lasker. And told me what to do once Tsering managed to shoot the arrow! Now quickly, stand aside," Cheojey implored. "I have my work to do."

As they moved aside, Cheojey took a vial from his robe. He opened it and threw the contents—a strange silvery powder that sparkled. It adhered to Raspahloh's bloody shirt. And then Raspahloh screamed.

To the Bonpo's champion, it was as if the powder Cheojey had thrown was liquid fire. Holding the arrow that was embedded deep in his chest with both hands, he groaned out, "You . . . kill . . . both . . . of us." Then his eyes rolled up and he lay limp, feeling weak as a kitten.

Dorjee rushed to his side. Whimpering, she lifted and cushioned his head on her hands. "Oh, what have you all done to him?"

Cheojey gently nudged her aside, and he grabbed the shaft. He pulled the arrow out, reciting mantras. Dorjee gasped—for normally the worst thing

225

you can do to a person with an arrow impaled in him is to remove it quickly. But there was no gushing blood issuing out of the gaping wound.

Cheojey softly said, "He will live. Baalzabub told us correctly. This is no *ordinary* arrow! Tsering, come here and bind him. As you know, there is much more to do!"

Tsering soon twisted their fallen enemy's hands behind his back, used some cut-off strands of the flywhisk to tie Raspahloh's hands. Shortly after, his feet were also bound. Raspahloh moaned and he awakened. He jerked at his bindings furiously. "Let me up," he snarled, crimson-faced, veins throbbing, "so I might kill you all!"

"Quickly—the sack!" Cheojey called out. "He must not see what I am about to do!" Tsering took out a black sack the Eden-tree occupant had provided. It was the size of a small tablecloth. He handed it to Cheojey, who snugged it down over Raspahloh's head. Amazingly, once this was done, Raspahloh quieted down.

"Next," explained the lama, "we must apply the other counter-measures. We have just minutes, or surely Lasker will be gone forever. Dorjee, you want to help, remove his shirt."

Dorjee tore Lasker's shirt from sleeve to sleeve, to bare the gaping wound from the arrow. Tears welled from her eyes. The wound was fearsome.

"Tear his sleeves open, too."

After she did so, Cheojey rubbed some more of the stuff that glittered like stardust on the chest wound. And as they watched, the wound *closed up*. The skin was repaired, as if it never had been pierced. Just as her finger had been replaced.

Cheojey took his robe-edge and used it to wipe away the blood. Then he dabbed more of the sparkly substance over the tattoos on Lasker's chest: Over the claws of the Snow Lion, and then on the Dragon-tattoos on Lasker's arms. "Have to cover all the marks on his body with this," Cheojey explained. "Help me roll him over."

They rolled Raspahloh over on his back, and Cheojey dabbed the substance over the tattoos there as well. The lama reached into his robe and extracted a bee-bee size golden object. Cheojey held it between two fingers and moved it along inches over the tattoos, as Baalzabub had instructed to do. Then once they turned him again, he repeated the procedure on Raspahloh's chest and arms.

"That's it, I think," Cheojey said proudly, standing up to admire his completed work. As they watched, the sparkly stuff began to smoke, and finally ignited. Raspahloh screamed and shouted, straining anew at his bindings, straining every mighty muscle to be released. That went on until the small flesh-fires died down. Amazingly, the skin was undamaged. The tattoos were brighter than ever, though.

The process of rescuing Lasker was not yet over. Raspahloh continued to struggle, and roared like a lion in captivity. Cheojey recited mantras of the Medicine Buddha, the others joining in. Dorjee's voice made the song beautiful and complete.

Raspahloh stopped struggling. He sagged and sighed, as if a great relief had engulfed him. His breathing came shallowly, weakly. Perhaps he was suffocating in the head-sack, Dorjee worried.

Dorjee broke the near-silence by asking, "Is he going to die?"

"No, he is restored," the lama said. "It is Lasker again. An exhausted, weak Lasker; breathing very shallowly. We must wait a bit."

They all sat down on the floor of the corridor, exhausted, no one even caring to step the few feet around the bend to see if the explosives had opened the way to the Great Skull's power-chamber.

"You can untie me now," Lasker said, in a calm, steady voice they all recognized. Dorjee rushed over to him, and removed the cloth from his head. He smiled and focused tired eyes on her.

Dorjee asked, "Is it really you?"

"Yes," Lasker said, "I don't know how you did it, but Raspahloh's gone."

After that, Cheojey peered into his eyes, took his pulses, and did some tests with the gold ball, holding it over Lasker's body, feeling it shift in his aura. In that way, Cheojey confirmed to himself it was not a trick. Lasker's retransformation was complete. They quickly unbound him, and Lasker rubbed at his ankles and wrists, wincing as circulation was restored. He took a little sip of water from the gourd canteen Dorjee handed him. She wet his still-feverish brow with a cloth torn from her blouse. Now was the time to ask questions.

"Where is Jade Jaguar?" Tsering asked. "Do you know?"

Lasker smiled. "He isn't the guy we thought he

228

was. Jade Jaguar isn't an Indian." Lasker went on to explain at some length that the Indian high priest was a Cultivator—the Guardian of the ship. And how the Guardian had vanquished the Bonpo. Lasker ended with the words, "I think Jadey-boy's gone back to his coffin."

"Good *riddance*," Rinchen said with emphasis. "Can't we finish our work and get the hell out of this place before more spooks appear?"

Dorjee said solemnly, "Bart—I'm so sorry. How awful it must be for you to have such a—thing—within. I wish with all my heart that now you are free of this affliction forever."

Lasker sighed. "For now, I am free of him. But I am sure Raspahloh still lurks inside." He rose up. "Rinchen's right. Let us get on with the task at hand. Come on, we'll see what the explosion has done."

Chapter Twenty-four

When the party reached the bulkhead, Lasker found that the explosives had blown a hole ten feet wide in the massive wall surrounding the heart of the Cultivators' great starship. And they beheld the seething blue energy skull! It was a bright, writhing mass floating like some sort of wizard's evil face above the floor of the chamber they had bared. Their hair stood out in the pounding of every beat. The great skull was a throbbing universe-dissolver, an anomaly in space-time held in stasis by unheard-of powers—powers that had to be extinguished if the Bonpo menace was to be stopped.

"See how it just *floats* there!" Dorjee exclaimed. "Oh, it is so beautiful, like some sort of huge flashing gem. I expected that it would be an ugly thing."

Lasker had to agree it was far from ugly. "It's not shaped like a human skull," he remarked. "It is more . . ." He didn't finish.

The Hermit harrumphed and harrumphed behind them. Yet they could not divert their attention from the glowing beauty before them. Finally the Cave-master said, "It is not intended to look like a human skull, but rather like the skull of a Cultivator, long and thin and noble. Only this is the *idealized* version of that skull. Perhaps they thought the most powerful thing in the universe should look like — *the face of God Himself.* So we would do well to look away," the Hermit cautioned. "Look *away.* Don't get drawn in. Already it is sucking you in!"

Lasker snapped out, "The Hermit is right. We're being drawn in. Avert your eyes, *now!*"

This was hardest to do for Lasker himself. He felt so powerfully drawn, like a moth to a flame, to the unearthly seething beauty of the thing that had been hidden for so many eons. Drawn by the beauty and because of the sheer *power* of it. This was the unimaginable essence of all matter and energy, a force sufficient to propel a craft a mile long through interstellar space! The skull star-drive was more a living thing than a machine. It was beyond both concepts — a swirling mass of negative and positive energy drawn from the fields of power between the stars themselves, drawn from the primordial stuff from which the universe was formed in the first nano-second of its existence!

Rinchen was the first to shake off the skull's siren spell, and jog his mind back to practical matters. "Let's get out of here! This is too — *weird!* Where's the cut-off switch?"

"I don't know where it is," Lasker said slowly, struggling at regaining control. "I don't think we should do too much monkeying with this."

"How else can we find the switch, without poking around?"

Lasker gave Rinchen a beaming look. "We'll get help!"

"Oh, no you're not." Rinchen snapped, "You're *not* going to—"

"Yes. We have to go find the Guardian and awaken him, if possible. Come on Rinchen; you weren't afraid of that little old Cultivator when you thought he was just a weird-looking Indian!"

"Not so," the big lug demurred, "I always had a healthy respect for the man—er, thing."

"Nevertheless, Lasker is right," the Hermit said. He was looking at a wall panel studying a bank of unlabeled dials. "Let us go see if the Guardian will help."

They made their way back along the corridor and to the coffin-chamber and found the lid repaired and closed. There didn't seem to be any way of raising it up. "Can't we pry it?" Dorjee asked.

"For the Gods' sake, let's get out of here," Rinchen said. He had taken a quick glance inside the coffin's glassine lid and seen that Jade Jaguar had stripped off his flesh like a false human face. There were six fingers ending on suction cups on each hand, and the skin was gray-blue all over his former drinking buddy. Rinchen shivered.

Lasker was not to be daunted. "I discovered some sort of hidden latch before. Ah, *here* it is. Well, here goes." He lifted the lid. A gaseous mist—very cold—swirled out, and then the big eyes popped open. Rinchen was backed against the far wall when the sleeper sat up.

"Oh, you are back? Your friends did succeed then."

"Yes," Lasker said. "And now we would ask you a favor. I remember your saying that the power of the Great Skull shouldn't be used for evil. But it is being used for that, still. There are more than one crystal skull-receivers in the hands of the Bonpo—and they will use their power against the world, bringing untold destruction, unless you help us deactivate the Great Skull."

The Cultivator yawned and stepped out of the coffin. "I must explain to you some facts. An accident—a systems malfunction—awoke me from my many thousand years of sleep about a hundred years ago. It also affected my memory, which is still faulty. I wandered out of the ship and quite forgot what I was all about at that time. I lived with the Indians who took me, as they took you, for some sort of god, or demi-god. Until I came here to the spacecraft with you, I'd even forgotten that I was the Guardian! Now I wish to do nothing but sleep. I hope to remember what I need to know in that great, long sleep. All I know now is that I was charged with the duty of protecting the field-drive—the 'skull' as you call it—from damage or misuse. Everything else is a blur. You will have to do what you do yourselves."

"Y-yes," Rinchen stuttered. "Let the, er, thing sleep. Let's get out of—"

"Guardian, we *will* do it ourselves," Lasker said, on sudden inspiration. "But come with us to the

234

chamber of the skull and tell us what we *shouldn't* touch—which dials and switches to avoid."

"I suppose I can do that, if I remember anything. You wish to turn it off . . . Yes! I remember! That is *good*. We are in Planet-fall. The drive should *not* be on. I think it is a malfunction that it is on."

"Good, then we are in agreement. Now, please, *come*."

The Guardian yawned again and said, "Very well," like a tired old person, and started to amble along with them. Rinchen kept as far away from his old drinking buddy as possible!

They reached the exploded-open chamber and Lasker said, "Okay—do any of these dials and thingamajigs turn it off?"

"I don't know," the Guardian said. "Can't remember."

"Think. At least tell us what dials not to turn."

The Guardian just stood there for a long time. Lasker almost expected the tall alien would scratch his head. But he didn't. Finally the Guardian said, "I can't remember."

Lasker, with exasperation, said, "Okay, so we all focus our minds on the task. Think—look everywhere. Can you walk around and look at all the dials with me, Guardian?"

But the Cultivator Guardian just sat down on the floor and lowered his head. "This is—strange to me. It is not . . . right that we are here. Yes . . . there is some sort of problem with being in the open with the skull before us so close. Not a physical danger, yet I don't know . . ." He trailed

235

off, staring at the floor.

Lasker felt sorry for the alien being. He was deprived of almost all the knowledge of his job, deprived of all his life memories, all connection to his friends up there in space. All he had left was to sit and feel empty. Emptier than any human could feel, for he had lost so much. An empire of stars!

Lasker shook the empathetic thought from his mind. He looked over the walls around the swirling energy mass. "There has to be a cut-off switch. It would look *important*. Touching the skull means annihilation. Even for Cultivators. But the cut-off switch has to be someplace *close* to the skull itself."

He gritted his teeth. "I'm going closer." He turned his back toward it. Being very careful of his footing on the smooth flooring, he backed toward the glowing blue throbbing force-field.

Carefully he counted his steps, stopping about four feet from the energy-mass. He started to walk around the object, keeping his back to the "face of God." He studied the brilliantly illuminated circular wall about the object. Nothing stood out. Just numberless dials! In a matter of a minute, he had made a full circle and had found nothing new. He went back to his friends.

"What now?" Tsering lamented. "To have come so far—faced so much, and be stymied like this . . ."

Cheojey had a suggestion. "Sit down a while," the medical lama said. "We are all worked up too much to see the answer. Too upset to think. We will find a way, if we meditate."

Lasker had to agree. In Tibet, Lasker knew, when you don't know what to do, you do *nothing*—for hours, sometimes days. He hoped in this instance that the meditation would be a matter of minutes.

"A very good idea," the Hermit said. "We'll come up with something." His bony hand squeezed Lasker's shoulder. "The Bonpo enemy is defeated. We can afford a few minutes to collect our ideas."

So they just got down and sat there cross-legged. Lasker sat closest to the Guardian, who remained immobile, presumably still trying to remember *something*.

Cheojey took the more difficult full-lotus position, keeping his back rigidly straight. The others sat Indian-style, cross-legged.

After a while Dorjee spoke up. "I remember something from my dream. There is something about the skull. It isn't whole."

"What?" Lasker asked, raising his eyes. "It looks whole."

"On . . . top," she said, smiling. "It is hollow. Inside. There is a hole on top of the head! And that has something to do with—whether it is on or off!" Dorjee had the solution! Or did she?

Except for the Guardian, they all got to their feet. "See?" smiled the lama, "patience creates new opportunities."

Lasker said, "I have to get on top of the skull. But how? I can't climb it." He looked around the ceiling above them carefully — and saw a small line, a hair thick. "There's some sort of trap door!" he exclaimed. "Rinchen, give me your hands — boost me up."

Rinchen did so, and Lasker found the catch on the trap door and pushed the four foot wide panel open. He peered inside. It was a crawlspace, leading over the room that held the power-skull. "I'm going in," Lasker said. Before anyone could object, he had crawled up into the space.

Chapter Twenty-five

Crawling on hands and knees, Lasker reached a hole over the Great Skull. There was a red metal rod like a fireman's pole extending down. He peered down along it, and saw that the pole didn't reach the hollow force-field swirling fifteen feet below. What did this all mean? Did the pole move up and down? Lasker examined the mechanism before him, and then shouted back, "I see a long rod coming down from the ceiling above me. It goes down almost into the hollow part of the field. If this thing is like an atomic pile—and I believe it is—this must be a *control* rod! If it's withdrawn, the power-field is on. If I can get it to descend—"

"What are you going to do?" The Hermit's voice, echoing down the passage, seemed worried.

"I'm going to try to push the rod *down*." Lasker crawled forward another few feet, ignoring the shouts from his friends not to attempt such a thing. Heaven knew, he didn't want to do it, *either!*

239

"I know I'm taking a chance, but what else can I do? The rod doesn't *touch* the force-field anywhere. It should be safe to touch. I hope."

"Wait," Cheojey said. "We will recite the mantra to destroy evil. If the Bonpo chant sent the rod *up* to activate the field, then our most ancient and holy mantra, given to us by Padmasambhava, must do the opposite."

"Go ahead and chant," Lasker said. "But we know that doesn't work! Don't all the Tibetan Buddhists chant that every morning? And yet the rod remains up. It must be stuck."

"Maybe if it is chanted closer," Cheojey said. His voice seemed right behind Lasker. Why, the old medical lama, too, had crawled up into the passage, Lasker saw, turning.

"Keep back, Cheojey. In case something happens here, I don't want you too close."

The lama started chanting, "DEMMA, DEMMA HRI-HO!" The sonorous chant immediately brought a response in the rod. It jerked and seemed to start to lower, then it caught on something. That happened repeatedly, like a stuck elevator door.

"Give up, Cheojey. I see the problem. There's a bent metal overhang interfering. Get back now. I'm going to grab ahold of the rod, pry it aside, to clear the mechanism."

"Don't touch it!"

"I already did and I'm still alive!" Lasker demanded that Cheojey retreat, and finally he did so.

Lasker worked carefully. He didn't want his at-

240

oms scattered about the universe any more than his friends wished that to happen! But with all his great power applied to the red rod to move it, it didn't move an inch. "No good," he said after minutes of exhaustive effort, "I'm coming back. I need a pry-bar of some sort."

Lasker crawled backward down the horizontal shaft and then felt Rinchen supporting his legs. He got back down in the corridor and looked around. "Is there a pipe, a stick of any . . . ?" And then his eyes alighted upon the Hermit's knobby walking stick. "Could I borrow your stick, Master?"

The Hermit said, "All right, but don't damage it. I made it myself out of very old—"

Lasker didn't let him finish. He took the stick and Rinchen boosted him into the passageway again.

Lasker again reached the open space over the skull force-field and the sticking rod. He started to push on the rod with the stick, as hard as he could. This time it started to give a bit.

But then everything he saw seemed to be bending, flattening out! The images before his eyes were flattening, as if he was staring into a swimming pool. It looked as if the Hermit stick was entering water! Visual distortion caused by the force-field! And Lasker had some odd thoughts, too. Images flashed before his mind's eye of—his own face staring at him bloodshot from the cracked medicine cabinet mirror of the Dil Praneth hotel. God, it was as if he was awakening from a week-long bender—Lasker was physically back in

241

his alcoholic New Delhi days!

After a while, his companions began to worry. "Are you all right, Bart?" It was Dorjee's voice, coming from the mirror.

Lasker shook off the images and shouted back, "I'm fine, but there's a strange field effect, I hope you can hear me. Your voice sounds really weird, like you're speaking very slowly, Dorjee."

"We can hear you fine," Tsering shouted into the access tunnel. "Can you dislodge the rod? Does the stick help?"

"Negative, but I'm still trying. It's tight. I'm almost directly over the damned energy-thing, and it's affecting me. I can look down into the power source. From here it looks like a swirling blue doughnut. There's no noise here, not even a hiss. Funny. I can sense raw *power*, it's as if I have a new sense— And I feel . . . All the power of the stuff that makes up the universe is here! I'm going to extend the Hermit's stick again now, try to pry . . . *Wow!*"

"What happened?" The Hermit's voice.

"Relax," Lasker called back, his own voice sounding tinny. "I saw my own face again, only very close up. Like in a funhouse mirror. Also, when I hold the stick forward, it seems to bend, like I'm putting it into water. This reality-warp stuff Baalzabub spoke about to me is real. I have trouble aiming the stick. I have to aim right, before I throw it."

"*Throw* it?" It was the Hermit's voice. "Don't damage that stick! I told you it's valuable."

"I'll whittle you another stick," Lasker shouted

back. "The world is at risk here; you'll have to sacrifice a little. I'm going to try to throw it down *into* the field—through the doughnut center. Maybe another object down there can reverse the field, just like the rod would have! Here goes . . . No! Wait! There's another problem. Hold on! I'll get back to you."

"What problem, Bart?"

Lasker couldn't answer the Hermit. The reality warp was becoming stronger and stronger. He was losing sight of his mission, his shape, even his ideas of who he was. The stick he held seemed like a long piece of pink taffy now. It was bending in a gentle breeze. Just like Lasker's mind was bending with the reality-warp around the Great Skull's power.

He looked at his hand and it appeared to be flat as a piece of paper, and a thousand miles long. He held a pancake with knobby bumps on it, not a stick. Then the hand was back to normal, but it held a broadsword, and the control rod that extended down before him vanished. Instead, it was a dragon. And he had to slay it. Lasker's mission was different. He had to . . . slay the dragon.

He tried to speak, to explain to the others that he was having some problems again, but the words seemed to be in a different language. Something that sounded like Middle English. He was no longer in the reality-tunnel he was used to, and it was most disconcerting. The very real and steamy-breathed dragon preened itself, digging teeth under shoulder scales to get at some annoying itch, apparently unaware of Lasker, who was out on a rock ledge in the Dragon's cavern . . .

"No! Can't be!" Lasker tried to keep a hold on his sanity. He had to remember what Baalzabub had said. What was it? He'd told Lasker to understand reality-tunnels. Everyone lived in a reality-tunnel, not a solid reality. Everyone wanted to cling to his own little arbitrary dream. To decide for himself what is real, despite all appearances, to be stubborn and just decide for himself what to believe was real. Yes that was it! Baalzabub said to understand reality is just a concept. To understand that when his senses said one thing, he could know another.

There *was no dragon*, and he was no knight with a broadsword in the dragon's lair!

Now the image changed before him. The Hermit's stick mutated before his eyes and became a long-stemmed flower. A beautiful, enormous red bloom! And he wasn't holding it, he was . . . he was the plant. Lasker was a plant, with a flower. Lasker was holding the part of him that was the flower up toward the sun. Not our sun! Instead, it was the enormous red sun of—a distant star system.

Plants don't think. How can I be thinking? Lasker thought.

Oh, yes they do think came his own reply. On this planet they do think! I am a philosophy plant! I sit in the sun and I speculate! I dream, I—think. That's funny . . . one of the things he was thinking was that he was something called a "Lasker," on some distant planet. He had crawled into a spaceship—something metal that went between stars. Was supposed to fix something.

How absurd! What a strange reverie . . . And yet . . . who is to say that reality is not as real as my reality here on XRstehTeu? The plant let itself speculate on this matter further. It even imagined some insectlike buzz that was telling it, "LLLAAAASSSKKKEEERRRR! AAARRREEE YYOOOUU OOKKKAAAYY??" And oddly enough, the plant understood those words. *Sure,* the plant thought, *I'm fine.* I just want to be who I am, the *best* philosophy-plant on XRstehTeu! I want to just soak up the sun and dream of . . . other things. Things like what some being had spoken to me once . . . by who?

The being's name was Baalzabub, and it had said, "Trust not your current concept of reality. Just follow the direction of your original mind. Follow your dream, that is as real as your reality.'

The philosophy-plant had another odd, yet amusing thought: If this ridiculous dream of being something called a Lasker, and trying to repair a spaceship's power source *were* as real as its own reality, then . . . what would happen? Why not dream some more about this? Might as well follow the dream . . .

It moved its flower upward, and the flower opened—a beautiful bloom. Then the philosophy-plant cried. Because the flower just turned into a dry stick that wasn't pretty at all. And it had to drop that stick through the force-field . . . reverse the force-field . . . whatever *that* was! And then It wasn't a plant anymore, it was . . . a Lasker!

"That's it!" Lasker said. "I am Bart Lasker, I am *not* a philosophy-plant!" With a twisting nausea, he fought the seductive other-reality away.

Whew! That had been a close call. That particular reality-tunnel was very seductive. The feeling of being a plant, sitting there . . . on that alien planet . . .

No, don't think of it again. Get to work. Disarm the force-field, before something else happens. He might not be so lucky next time, Lasker told himself. Next time the reality-tunnel he entered could be of something that didn't think at all! Then how could he ever return?

He moved the stick again, aiming it down at the hole in the swirling doughnut of energy. His aim had to be perfect. Lasker threw it. As it descended, it took on the appearance of a snake, then a flower—the same flower he had once been. Then it went into the swirling force-field and the stick became Lasker.

There was a brilliant flash. Did the universe explode? Everything was spinning, and he was shouting; shouting in glee.

He was under a crystal-cold waterfall with Dorjee. Oh, how he wanted to be in this reality, not plunging through an interstellar drive-field, being torn into atoms.

The waterfall changed into flames. He screamed, and then the flames became a narrow passageway he had to crawl along. Why?

"Are you allright!" Cheojey was leaning over him, looking down rather anxiously. "You've been babbling for a half hour. Feel better?"

"Yes . . . What happened?"

Tsering moved Cheojey aside. "I think you've done it, Bart," the rebel chief exclaimed. "You've cut off the power on the Great Skull."

Lasker sat up and with his companions began watching the swirling God-face before them grow dimmer and less active, until it just barely glowed, like the afterglow of a shut-off television's picture tube.

"Where's my stick?"

"I don't know, Hermit," Lasker replied, annoyed. "Perhaps it's in some other galaxy."

"*Bah,* it was a good stick, too! Oh, well, everything has a time," the Hermit chuckled. "So. Now the Bonpo crystal skulls will not pick up any power. It is over at last. We can go home. Chalk another one up for the Mystic Rebel!"

"Yes, home," Rinchen snorted. "And about time at that!"

Dorjee held Lasker close and smoothed his hair, which was standing straight up, like it was electrically charged. As she kissed him, Lasker's mind momentarily flashed to other times, other places. The alternate realities, the things he had *been* during his moments over the force-field. The flash-vision of Dorjee and him swimming in the cold water of the waterfall returned to him—and the insane vision of being the philosophy-plant. And

247

then he remembered the flames of an imaginary hell that he had been taught to believe in in his childhood. A hell that never had, and never would, exist. He should know.

Kisses returned him to the present. He broke away to ask, "Where's Jade Jaguar?"

The Hermit said, "He's napping again."

Lasker smiled, "He has quite a reality-tunnel, doesn't he?"

They all looked at him, perplexed.

Chapter Twenty-six

Clouds of sandalwood incense wafted through the tranquil, vast marble meditation room at the second level of the Dalai Lama's palace in Dharmsala. Things were going on much as usual. The morning ablutions were being observed. The monks, some skinny recent escapees from Communist tyranny in Tibet, old beyond their years; others monks raised in the freedom of the West, well fed smooth-skinned, youthful, took their places on their red meditation cushions.

The *gekko* pinged the small bell, and they all began to sing the same mantra the Tibetans had recited for at least a thousand years. A chant composed, some said, by Lord Padmasambhava himself. Or as others said, learned by the great saint in his epic journey to Shambhala: "DEMMA, DEMMA HRI-HO! DEMMA, DEMMA HRI—HO!"

Lungpo Rinpoche was *gekko*—meditation leader—today. The Dalai Lama, high on his pedestal throne before the monks, listened for an hour, then nodded to give the cue. Lungpo loudly began to intone the second recitation: "MHARI OM SHI-VAYA HRI! PADMA SAVA GRESHI-HUM!" Other monks hit their little drums with balls of lead.

The usual.

Lungpo didn't feel very alert this A.M. He could barely stifle a yawn when the chant stopped and all began silent meditation. And his leg hurt, too. Perhaps it was time to see Lama Drogang again for some more Eagle-22 antiarthritic concoction. His mind drifted. He had to open his eyes slightly and raise their focus from the floor in order to not fall dead asleep!

Dawn was breaking over the mountains to the east. Blue, red and yellow rays — the Tibetan flag colors. This was a good omen for sure — a most auspicious omen. Lungpo adjusted his legs to be slightly askew of perfect lotus-position. Compassion over form, isn't that what they said? And compassion for *oneself* was just as important, wasn't it? Why injure his legs?

Again he drifted. Catching himself, he prodded himself on the knee with a sharp index fingernail, to keep awake. How many more minutes left?

Keeping the mind alert, yet unfocused on anything during meditation was important, he reminded himself. It was necessary to abide in nothingness for an hour after reciting the great Padmasambhava mantra. Especially at morning *puja,* when you sat before the great Avilokteshvara — compassion God, the Dalai Lama, you try to look good.

Such a sleepy morning. He yawned. And so warm! Why, it was so warm, wouldn't even a good meditator be off stride today? Aside from the rays of the rising sun's color, so very ordinary. The Dharma—the true doctrine—stated that everything changes. But nothing seemed a bit different today. Except his leg, that is. That got worse and worse! When would this be over?

Suddenly, there was another color. It permeated the sky. The other monks saw it, too. A bright white flash to the north, a blue afterglow—coming from Tibet. He looked to the Dalai Lama. Was he disturbed, too?

His Holiness had turned his head, an unusual event in meditation, and stared out beyond the red sandstone pillars and smiled. He seemed to almost chortle, rocking in his position. He was happy. Lungpo caught the smile and the wink. Something *good* had happened. Something great and wonderful.

The meditation continued.

And the dawn became cherry red—brilliant. For weeks, it had been occulted with a sickly greenish tinge. That was gone now.

What had happened?

The Dalai Lama *still* smiled—only now it was an inward smile. He was absolutely mirthful. Why, the month of meditation on the problem of the Bonpo had finally paid off. This morning the Padmasambhava chant for the cutting off of energy to the evil ones had worked. The flash of light was a last burst of dying energy from the Great Skull. The green power of the world's enemies had faded.

How had this happened? He let his mind roam—not "mind" in the conventional sense, but the wisdom-mind of the *third eye*—the omnipotent voyager in time-space. He searched for the source of the change—and found it. Down below—the vibration of a great hero of the dharma.

The Mystic Rebel had been the instrument of the event! Bart Lasker, the American fated to join the cause of Tibet, had succeeded again.

Such joys, like sorrow, are ephemeral. This was a temporary gain for the side of the Light of the World. But only temporary. All phenomena are as ephemeral as the seasons.

His Holiness drew back his third eye and shook the *vajra*-bell to end the meditation.

Epilogue

High atop Mt. Kailas, in the snowswept Tibetan heights, a misty kingdom not-quite-of-this-earth had been shaken to the core. The headquarters of the Bonpo sorcerers was ruled now by fear.

How could it be? Zompahlok had failed.

The minions of evil bowed before the great black-and-gold many-armed statue of Yamantalai, which was holding pieces of their offering of human bodies—in its hands. The crystal-skull necklace of the Great One, Yamantalai, Lord of Death, had stopped glowing green! The crystal skulls had become inert, powerless. Dark, cloudy ornaments, and no more! "Woe to this day," the supplicants chanted. "For Zompahlok is no more."

Then, before their cowled faces, a misty form coalesced. "I cannot be destroyed," hissed Zompahlok as he solidified. He stepped forward, enraged at this spectacle of his followers believing not in him.

He sat down on his throne of skulls and twisted his skeleton ring around and around his index finger, lost in thought as the supplicants rushed this way and that, to their tasks. He thought, *Something unique has happened. I have been discorporated by some weapon of the great ancient ones — by one of the Cultivators himself! This intervention of the space-born can be the only reason I failed to prevent the shutdown of the power of our crystal skulls. Yet — is this loss final?*

Zompahlok stood and called for his chief aide, who materialized before him and bowed.

"What do you wish I do?" Phunstock asked.

"Do? We will gather the others, say the activating chant again. If the source has been turned off — perhaps we can turn it on — again!"

Under Zompahlok's direction, the dry-bodied Bonpo magicians gathered before the great statue. They chanted many variations of the activating mantra — for hours. All to no avail!

"Enough," Zompahlok hissed, finally. "Go and maintain your rounds! The tide of battle will turn again, this I pledge."

He sat alone again on his skull-throne before the flickering central green fire of the temple and raged. His anger knew no bounds. He beseeched the great Yamantalai, "Give me power!" He said it over and over, until he collapsed onto the green stone tiles in exhaustion. The great lord of death had not given a sign.

"What do we do now?" he asked himself. And then he raised up and intoned, "It is not over yet! The Bonpo cause has done without the crystal skull-powers before. All is not lost. I will plan. I will think."

Zompahlok slumped back down on the throne built-of-skulls and pondered. After a long while, his corpse-dry lips pursed in a slight smile. One power was gone, a great power. But it wasn't defeat. With just the primeval sorcery they had used for centuries, the Bonpo had almost defeated the Buddhists many times. The dark kingdom was yet gathering strength. It was written that they would succeed. There were other powers to be tapped! One power not yet his was a power stronger than the crystal skull. All he had to do was find a way to seize it. His cracked lips parted in a slight smile. That power existed right in the midst of the Tibetan Buddhists themselves, and yet they knew not to use it! If it could be stolen . . . If there could be found a way . . .

He reached out to a vase, pulled up a black rose, and crushed it in his hand. It shattered like glass, and fell to the floor beneath his skull-throne. The pattern of the shattered petals fell to resemble a snake.

It was the sign! The great Demon-Lord had given a sign!

The Serpent Power would be his. Very soon!

BLOCKBUSTER FICTION FROM PINNACLE BOOKS!

THE FINAL VOYAGE OF THE S.S.N. SKATE   (17-157, $3.95)
by Stephen Cassell
The "leper" of the U.S. Pacific Fleet, SSN 578 nuclear attack sub SKATE, has one final mission to perform—an impossible act of piracy that will pit the underwater deathtrap and its inexperienced crew against the combined might of the Soviet Navy's finest!

QUEENS GATE RECKONING   (17-164, $3.95)
by Lewis Purdue
Only a wounded CIA operative and a defecting Soviet ballerina stand in the way of a vast consortium of treason that speeds toward the hour of mankind's ultimate reckoning! From the bestselling author of THE LINZ TESTAMENT.

FAREWELL TO RUSSIA   (17-165, $4.50)
by Richard Hugo
A KGB agent must race against time to infiltrate the confines of U.S. nuclear technology after a terrifying accident threatens to unleash unmitigated devastation!

THE NICODEMUS CODE   (17-133, $3.95)
by Graham N. Smith and Donna Smith
A two-thousand-year-old parchment has been unearthed, unleashing a terrifying conspiracy unlike any the world has previously known, one that threatens the life of the Pope himself, and the ultimate destruction of Christianity!

Available wherever paperbacks are sold, or order direct from the Publisher. Send cover price plus 50¢ per copy for mailing and handling to Pinnacle Books, Dept.17-307, 475 Park Avenue South, New York, N.Y. 10016. Residents of New York, New Jersey and Pennsylvania must include sales tax. DO NOT SEND CASH.